KEY L

ISLAMORADA

MARATHON

BIG PINE KEY &
THE LOWER KEYS

KEY WEST

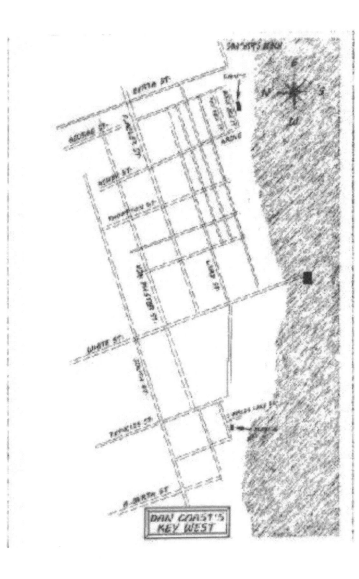

DAN COAST'S
KEY WEST

Sleeping Dogs Lie

From the Tales of Dan Coast

Sleeping Dogs Lie
From the Tales of Dan Coast

By

Rodney Riesel

Published by Island Holiday Publishing
East Greenbush, NY

Special thanks to:

Jimmy Buffett
His music turned clouds into sunshine,
Snow into sand,
Work boots into flip flops,
and most importantly helped me understand that
the beach was just as much attitude as latitude.
and to
US 1 Radio 104.1 FM
Key West, Florida
For helping me start every morning in a Key West state of mind.

Cover and maps designed by:
Connie Fitsik

To obtain more copies of this book
"Like" *Sleeping Dogs Lie* at
facebook.com/rodneyrieselsleepingdogslie

For Brenda,
Kayleigh, Ethan
& Peyton

Chapter One

It was a beautiful day. The kind of day one would compare to the word, *paradise*. Sunny, a few clouds dotting the sky, but the kinds of clouds that move across the sky slowly, never seeming to move in front of the sun. It was seventy-five degrees, and a light breeze blew off the ocean rustling the palm trees. The clean salt air was refreshing. Gulls flew overhead and cried out. An air horn blew in the distance. Waves crashed against the beach. It was like a dream, a memory.

A man and a woman stood in the front yard of a modest beach house, next to a sign that read, "For Sale." The home was a one-story bungalow, white with green shutters. The dormer in the front gave the illusion of a second story, but there was none.

A short gravel driveway led up to the house, and a pathway of the same material led from the driveway to the front steps. Sitting planted in the front yard were two palm trees, and next to the road was a mailbox mounted on a post. On top of the mailbox were painted the numbers 632. The front steps led to a porch, completely enclosed in a metal, slightly rusted screen.

The couple were holding hands and facing the front of the house. The woman was grinning at the joke the man had just told about a real estate agent and a farmer's daughter.

"That's bad," she said.

"I didn't write it," he responded.

"No, but you told it. That makes you just as bad as the guy who wrote it."

"Where the hell is she?" he asked, "We said three-thirty."

"She'll be here. Calm down, Boob."

They both turned toward the road as they heard a car pull up across the street. It was a shiny new Porsche, dark blue, with the top down. The car skidded to a stop half in the road and half on the neighbor's lawn.

"I think her commission is too high," he said to his wife.

"You drive a Porsche," she returned.

"I'm rich, bitch," he responded, laughing. She playfully kicked his shin.

A woman climbed out of the car, a Clorox-blonde woman. Deeply tanned, some sun with a lot of bed mixed in. She was not old, but probably too old for the pony-tail through the Marlin's ball cap she was sporting. She wore bright red lipstick, a shirt that appeared to be one size too small. The top two buttons were purposely undone, probably after she left the house in the morning. She was not the most beautiful woman in the world, but it was a sure bet that her husband thought she was. Especially in the Daisy Duke shorts she was wearing this afternoon.

"I wonder if this is the real estate agent, or the farmer's daughter?" he speculated to his wife.

"Be nice," she warned.

"You must be the Coasts," the agent said, holding out her hand.

"Yes. I'm Alex, and this is Dan," Alex said, reaching out to accept the saleswoman's hand.

"I'm Emily Dixon. Sorry I'm late. Did you have a look around the property?"

"Yes we did, it's beautiful. The palm trees, the view. It's just what we were looking for," Alex replied.

"Try not to sound so eager," Dan said to his wife. "I was going to try and offer them less."

"I don't think they would take any less, Mr. Coast." Emily said matter-of-factly.

"Well not now they wouldn't." he said, as he glared at his wife.

"Places like this are in big demand and going pretty fast right now. This is a decision that won't wait, Mr. Coast…Mr. Coast…?"

*****

"Mr. Coast… Mr. Coast?" she asked, shaking his leg, "Are you awake?"

"Wha, what the Christ do you want?"

"Are you Dan Coast?" she asked.

Dan Coast lay face down in a hammock, his black tee shirt and tan cargo shorts wrinkled. Dan's long arms hung over the sides of the hammock, his knućkles touching the sand. Dan lay there staring through the net at an empty bottle that lay next to his Ray Ban sunglasses. Dos Manos, the bottle read. *Good God. Did I drink that, or did someone hit me in the head with it? There's no blood dripping into the sand, I guess I must have drank it.*

"Yeah, I'm Coast. What do you want?" he answered.

Coast slowly turned his head toward the voice, rubbing his eyes, his mind slowly transferring from dream to reality. His face had the slight imprint of the hammock netting. His blue eyes were blood shot from a long night of alcohol abuse, and around his eyes the crow's feet showed his age. Laugh lines some people call them, and that may be the way Dan's started out. In recent years however they were due to long nights, too much booze, and squinting at paradise's sun. Most days the lines on his face were not so prominent, but these rough nights made them more noticeable.

"Someone told me you could help me," she replied.

"Yeah, who?"

"He said he was a good friend of yours."

Well that narrowed it down to about six from an island of twenty-three thousand. Coast didn't have a lot of friends. He had acquaintances. He had drinking buddies. He had people he worked for. He had people who worked for him. But he didn't consider any of them friends. Some of them probably considered him a friend, and that was fine with Dan. He had learned long ago that more good came from being liked, than it did from liking someone.

He pulled himself up out of the hammock with a groan. *Jesus Christ*, he thought, *you never heard Gilligan or Skipper bitch about their back, and they slept in a hammock every night.*

Dan stood by the hammock trying to subtly stretch different parts of his five foot, eleven inch body.

First his neck, and back, then his wide shoulders and legs. If his uninvited guest didn't notice the stretching, she surely heard the cracking of bone. Dan's mentality and sense of humor may have still been that of a teenage boy, but the rest of him wasn't getting any younger. The creaking and cracking were a new language his body had learned in the last few years. Its way of telling him he was old. Too old to stay up drinking in a local bar all night, and definitely too old to sleep in a hammock all night. Dan heard what his body was telling him, and even thought it might believe it, but convincing Dan was going to take a few more years at least. Although Dan was beginning to feel the effects of aging in recent years, he was still in pretty good shape on the outside. He was in his mid-forties, but if he laid off the booze for a few days, he could easily pass for a man in his mid-thirties, but he didn't lay off the booze often. A slight belly had formed, but nothing he couldn't suck in and hold when the right woman strolled by, and most times that woman looked back and smiled. His hair was starting to turn grey, but he told himself it was turning grey in all the right spots. He told himself he looked distinguished. Dan's hair had thinned a little, but lately he was getting it cut shorter, thinking no one would notice.

"Help you how?" he asked.

"My friend is missing," she replied.

"Boyfriend?" Dan asked, already knowing the answer.

"Yes, boyfriend."

"Maybe he just got sick of you and went back to the mainland. You know, that happens a lot down here. The girl thinks they are soul mates, the boy gets down here and sees what a woman is supposed to look like in a bikini, and he goes crazy. The women are a little younger, a little browner, and in a lot better shape. No offense."

"None taken," she responded in a not too convincing tone. "Go on."

"Sometimes he shacks up with one of these beauties for a few days and then comes back with his tail between his legs. Sometimes he's never seen again. Sometimes he just goes home," Dan finished.

"That's some speculation, Mr. Coast. You really know how to make a woman feel special." She said.

She was right, Dan was being a prick. A mood brought on by a lousy night's sleep, too much alcohol, and being shot down in front of a bar full of people by a twenty-four-year-old stewardess. A stewardess that seemed pretty interested earlier in the night but lost most of that intrigue as Dan grew drunker, louder, and more obnoxious as the evening progressed. Dan could be charming when sober, but sometimes he took a turn in the other direction when drunk. Now Dan was taking his anger and frustrations out on this woman, a woman who came to ask him for help. She just seemed to remind Dan a little too much of last night's stewardess. This woman too had blonde hair; she was tall, thin. It was obvious she took good care of herself, exercised, ate right. She also had that same tone of voice as the stewardess. That way of speaking and moving that let you know she was just a little bit smarter than you, a little bit better. Dan didn't like people who acted like that, and he could feel himself not liking this woman very much.

"Hey, I'm just saying," Dan continued, "maybe he's not missing. Maybe he knows exactly where he is, and exactly what he wants, and maybe what he wants is to not be found."

"He wouldn't have left without me, and he sure wouldn't have left me for someone else. At least not yet," she said.

"I'm not so sure about that. I've known you for about five minutes and…ah never mind. How long has this guy been missing?" Dan asked, mustering as much sincerity as his sarcasm would allow.

"Since Wednesday, around two pm. We were lying by the pool. A hotel employee came out and told him there was a call for him at the front desk. He went in to answer it, and that's the last time I saw him." As she finished speaking, she took a deep breath and moisture appeared at the corners of her eyes.

"So, to make a long story short, two days? When did you get here to the island?"

"Late Monday night," she explained. "We left Miami right after my husband's funeral."

"Like sands through the hourglass," he whispered to himself.

"What?" she snapped.

"Nothing. Listen, I'll see what I can do. I'm not going to guarantee that I'll find him, but I get paid either way. Up front and in cash. Is that going to be a problem?

"That won't be any problem at all, Mr. Coast," she replied.

"It's Dan. Meet me at Red's at three, it's a small bar on Charles Lake Road. I have a few more questions and we'll discuss the amount of the payment."

She agreed, thanked him, turned, and walked briskly away.

Dan didn't need the money. It's not that he already had too much; he just didn't need any more. His winnings got him everything he wanted. Well, almost everything. He still had neighbors who bugged him, they still borrowed things, their dogs still barked at night. It's just now his neighbors were a little browner, a little less clothed, and they never needed to borrow his snow shovel. Even though he didn't need the money, he still liked to get paid. He tried living off his winnings when he first arrived, fishing, lying on the beach, drinking, but that got old real fast. All but the drinking, that is.

Dan had been self-employed in his old life back on the mainland. Just like his father before him, he was a carpenter, mostly doing home improvements and remodeling jobs. He was used to working hard, and he was used to getting paid. Some habits die hard.

He watched as she walked across the yard, hips swaying, and up the gravel pathway toward the front

17

of his house. Now that his head had started to clear a little from the tequila fog, he noticed how good she looked, and why she had had one too many men in her life. *Wow, she looks good from behind, not too bad from the front either. It's funny though, how annoying can turn a 10 into a 7. Crap, what was her name?*

Dan started to call out to her. *What should I call out*? he wondered, *Ma'am, Miss, Hey, annoying lady? Ah forget it. I'll see her at Red's later anyway. Then she'll tell me her name. And if she doesn't show up, then it doesn't matter anyhow.*

He rubbed his eyes, his head, and stretched his arms toward the tops of the palm trees. He bent over and touched his toes. Then stood back up straight and cracked his neck from side to side. With a heavy drop he sat back down, laid back, and gazed up at the tops of the palm trees.

That was a tough workout, I'm going to need a little power nap.

Coast closed his eyes. He wasn't used to being woken up this early after a long night out. It had been a long time since there had been someone to wake him up, and even longer since there was a good reason to be up. After moving to the island, Dan's motto had pretty much become, "If God wanted everything done now, he wouldn't have put so many numbers on the clock."

Chapter Two

Dan awoke a few hours later to the sound of laughter. He was looking up at the same palm trees that he had closed his eyes to. The headache was still there, a little nausea. The sun was a little brighter now. He rolled over and searched the sand below for his sunglasses. *Must have caught some kind of mezcal flu or something, h*e thought cynically.

Then the laughter again. He could hear it was a young girl and guy. Young, but not as young as they were acting. Dan raised his head to see who was trespassing on his own personal hangover. *Tourists. Of course, it's always just-fell-off-the-brochure tourists that laugh the loudest.*

It was a girl in her mid-twenties, and a guy about the same age. Their faces were identically sunburned. They were running up and down the beach playing grab ass the way young lovers do. She would try to catch him, and then he would try to catch her. When one caught the other, they would hug and kiss, and laugh, sometimes falling into the sand arm in arm.

Dan sat at the edge of his hammock; eyes squinted behind the sunglasses that weren't quite doing their trick. As he sat alone in the morning sun, watching the horny couple frolic, he felt almost embarrassed, spying on them as he was. He looked around to see if anyone was watching him as he watched them. Even though he felt some kind of joy seeing the way they held each other, the way they spoke, and looked into each other's eyes, he told himself he was annoyed, and acted as such. Then he heard her say it: "This is beautiful, I would love to live here."

Dan shook his pounding head and instantly regretted his actions.

"That's the first time I ever heard anyone say that", Dan called out to the couple.

"What?" the young man yelled back.

"Nothing, never mind, I thought you were someone else", Dan responded.

"*Someone who isn't bugging the crap outta me*", he wanted to yell.

A moth-eaten debate raged in Dan's mind. *Why is it everyone thinks they would love to live here? Haven't any of these people heard the old saying, "It's a great place to visit, but I wouldn't want to live there?" Can't they see that the smiles on the visitor's faces are always a lot bigger than the smiles, if any, on the locals?*

But Dan knew the answers to these questions that he presented himself, even if he did ask them over and over again. In the back of his mind he remembered. He remembered a lot of things. He remembered the first time he came to the beach, to the ocean with a special woman. He remembered running along in the sand playing grab ass. He remembered falling arm and arm into the soft Florida sand for the first time. He remembered the first time he heard a Jimmy Buffett song on the radio, while sitting in a tiki hut having drinks with his grab ass partner. He remembered when falling asleep in a hammock was just a dream. All of these memories were etched in his mind forever, right alongside that memory of himself saying, "This is beautiful, I would love to live here."

Now here he was, living here, but more passing out in a hammock than falling asleep in it. The young girl on the beach was right though, it was a great place to live. Dan just never thought he would be doing it alone. But he was alone, alone on his hammock, alone in his yard. Dan's yard was mostly sand with a few patches of sand reed scattered about. It had a slight slope down toward the beach. There were three palm trees in the yard, two supporting the hammock, and a third a few feet away from them next to a small green shed that Dan used as a wood shed. In the middle of the yard was a small fire pit. Next to the fire pit were two Adirondack chairs that faced the beach. There was a gravel pathway leading from the fire pit that split into a Y with one path leading to a set of steps going up to

Dan's back door, and the other winding its way around the house to the driveway and onto the street. On each side of the back steps there were flower boxes that Dan had built a while back, planted with bougainvillea, and then abandoned soon after.

Dan got up off the hammock and lumbered across the sand and up the gravel pathway to his back door, his headache and nausea in tow. He walked through the screen door, into the kitchen, poured a cold cup of yesterday's coffee from the pot, put it in the microwave, and set it to one minute.

Other than the microwave and coffee pot, anyone entering Dan's kitchen would think they had just time traveled back to 1975. The cabinets were metal, painted a deathly white over and over numerous times. The sink was white cast iron sitting atop a baby shit yellow Formica countertop. The walls were lime green, and the appliances looked like they were picked up at Carol Brady's garage sale.

Dan's plan had been to remodel the kitchen, as well as the other rooms, but that plan had been put on hold along with a lot of others.

He walked down the short hallway that led to two bedrooms, and at the end, the bathroom. He rested the palms of his hands on the sink and stared into the mirror. As his own world-weary eyes looked quizzically, almost challengingly, back at him, his mind began to wander. His eyes told a story that he hoped only he could read. There was always something to remind him, always something to make the memories come flooding back. This morning it just happened to be a young couple on the beach, running, laughing, and wishing the same things he had once wished.

He began to think back, as he so often did. Back to another life, another time, another place. It seemed like so long ago, but the smallest reminder could make the pain feel so fresh. It always amazed Dan how easy it was to mask the pain. A few drinks, a few jokes, and no one knew what was on the inside, only the happy-go-lucky, sarcastic facade. Always calling attention to others instead of to himself.

Dan turned on the cold and stuck his head under the running water for a few seconds, splashed water on his face, grabbed a towel and dried off. *"Ding!"* Coffee's ready.

He walked back into the kitchen, grabbed the coffee, and drank it down, along with four aspirins. By this time the headache was almost gone, as well as the nausea.

There was a time in Dan's life when a hangover would have lasted all day. Not anymore though. Tolerance has its rewards, and Dan had spent a lot of the last few years building up that tolerance. Red's was his gym, and glasses of tequila were his dumb bells. He was slowly turning into an Olympic drinker.

Dan looked from the kitchen into the living room at the flannel, red and purple dog bed in the corner. The bed was puffy, fluffed up high. Dan could tell Buddy had not slept in it the night before. *Someone got lucky last night.* It was at that moment that Dan caught an unholy whiff of himself and winced. *Either the neighbors are making chicken soup, or I need a shower.*

Chapter Three

As Dan stood in his shower, leaning against the front wall letting the cool water run over his head and down his back, he heard what had become a familiar sound coming from outside his bathroom window. A sound that shouldn't be loud enough to hear from the house next door. Especially over the sound of running water. It was two people in a heated exchange. One male, one female. The female he knew well. She was a friend. She was one of the first people Dan had met upon his arrival to Key West. Her name was Bev.

Bev was in her late fifties, but one of those late fifties that looked early forties, with a certain way about her that was early twenties. Bev was blonde, probably not natural at this point, but at one time probably. She always wore her hair up like one of those Bond girls back when Connery was Bond, and she had the curves to match.

Her husband was Frank, but this wasn't Frank doing the yelling. Frank had passed away about a year ago at the unripe age of fifty-seven. He was one of those men that Dan described with no irony whatsoever as, "A great guy."

Dan had met Frank and Bev the first night he moved in. It was late on a Thursday night. He had had enough of unpacking, rearranging, and situating, when he decided to build his first fire in his new fire pit and start in on the bottle of Johnny Walker he had purchased earlier that day. It was one of those quiet evenings Dan hated, no noise to drown out your own thoughts.

As he sat in one of the two old Adirondack lawn chairs that had come with the place, staring out at the ocean, two people approached from the house next door halfway through his third drink.

"All moved in?" the man asked.

Dan choked out the word "yes" as he wiped his eyes and tried quickly to regain his composure. It may have been a tear brought on by a distant memory, or it may have been the salt in the air.

"We don't usually introduce ourselves, but we saw the U-Haul trailer and figured you were staying for more than a week. Did you buy the place?" the woman asked.

"Yes, yes I did," Dan replied.

"That's great. While it was a rental, we never knew what we were going to get from week to week.

College kids, bikers, church group, or a family of ten," she said chuckling.

"Is there a missus or is it just you?" the man asked.

"Just me, pretty much," said Dan.

"Well, I'm Frank, and this is my lovely bride, Bev," Frank said, extending his hand.

"It's a pleasure to meet you," Dan said smiling, taking Frank's hand and giving it a slight shake. Frank was only taller than Dan by about two inches, but when Dan stood next to Frank he felt small. Hale and hearty, genuinely warm and friendly, Frank just had that larger than life presence. He had a full head of white hair, thinning a little at the crown and temples, but certainly more hair than most men his age. Frank always had a smile on his face, and the attitude that made you think, *this man's never had a bad day in his life*. Dan was over a thousand miles from his own father, but felt closer to him when Frank was nearby.

Over the next year and a half, Dan, Frank and Bev became great neighbors, friends, and drinking buddies. Frank was always good for a joke, and the same jokes were always good. It always amazed Dan how Frank could tell the same stories over and over again, and still make them interesting and funny.

Whether the story was about Frank's time in the Merchant Marines, his twenty-two years in the Air Force, or his stories about doing time in Catholic school with "Sister Oleo Margarine" cracking the ruler across his knuckles. To Dan, Frank was one of those few people you meet in life that make your life better. Not just Frank, but also his wife of almost forty rompin', stompin' years. Frank's words, not Dan's.

But the stories and the jokes all came to a sudden halt about a year ago. Bev was at the grocery store picking up that night's supper, and Frank had brought his kayak down to the water for a quick paddle up to the beach and back. Frank always said these regular trips were for his health, but Bev knew it was more for the scenery. The nineteen and twenty year old, female scenery. She didn't mind. She just referred to Frank as a dirty old man.

On that particular day Dan was sitting in his back yard having a cocktail and reading that morning's edition of the Key West Citizen, the local daily paper, as Frank walked by with his kayak above his head, singing a ditty about a skipper and his cabin boy. A song Dan had heard many times over the last year and a half. Frank looked over at Dan, smiled, and nodded. Dan grinned and returned the nod. Frank put his kayak in the water, climbed aboard, and paddled away.

An hour or so later Frank returned, beached his kayak, climbed out, picked it up over his head, and started walking back up to the house. He made it about halfway when he felt a sudden stabbing pain in his head. He laid the kayak down beside him, stood back up while rubbing the side of his head, and looked toward the house. Bev was in the kitchen window. Their eyes met, and Frank gave her a big smile. Then his knees buckled, and he fell to the sand. Bev ran to her husband's side, dropped to her knees, and called out his name. She gently shook him, as if trying to wake him from a nap. Frank didn't wake up; he died there in Bev's arms.

The funeral, as well as the next few months, following Frank's stroke were pretty rough on Bev. She had lost the only man she had ever loved. They never had children, so she was all alone.

Dan went over to the house as much as he could. He would try to help out around the place. He would invite Bev over for drinks, but she never came. She had become withdrawn, that is, until the last few months.

While walking on the beach one afternoon she had met a man about her age, his name was Don. Don was a local man, born and raised in the Keys. Don was well known, mostly by bartenders. He never kept a job for more than a couple of years. Sometimes he would just quit showing up for work, but most of the time he was fired. In every instance he would always have a convenient story that convinced no one about how it wasn't his fault, it was his boss's. Every time Don was fired it had something to do with his temper. That at least was true.

Bev and Don struck up a conversation in that first meeting, and in Bev's eagerness to end her loneliness, they began spending more and more time together. First lunches, then dinners, and eventually sleepovers.

Within two months Don was living with Bev. It didn't take much convincing on his part, especially when he found out how much money Frank had left his beloved. Don was the kind of man that Dan described as a real asshole, but their "romance" had progressed far too quickly for the heartsick Bev to notice Don's faults.

It wasn't long after they moved in together that Bev finally started to notice things about Don that everyone else in town already knew. Don was a drinker, and not a friendly one by any means. After a few weeks the yelling started. At first the arguments were once every couple of weeks, and then once a week. Don would get drunk, and then accuse Bev of sleeping around. This, compounded by Bev's increased drinking of late, made for a volatile mixture. On more than one occasion, when Don had left the house after an argument, Dan went over to see if Bev was alright. She would tell him everything was fine, and not to worry about her, but Dan did worry. Frank had been a good friend, and Dan felt that he owed it to him to keep an eye on things now that he was gone.

As Dan stepped out of his shower, he grabbed a towel, and went to the window. He looked to the house next door that had once been a happy place filled with love and laughter. He saw Don coming out of the front door, slamming it behind him. Dan looked to each window, and then saw Bev walking out the back door, crying. He closed the curtains.

Chapter Four

Clean, showered, but unshaven, as usual, Dan climbed into his car. It was once a great car, a 2006 Porsche 911 Carrera convertible. Now, not so great. One alcohol induced dent after another, covered in primer to reduce the effects of rusting, and never being washed had turned Dan's once beautiful lottery winning memento into a pile of rolling shit.

The car was dark blue, Dan's favorite color. What had the salesman called it? Cerulean. The same color blue as the two stripes on each side of the palm tree that sat in Dan's front yard. The same color blue as the side of his porch, as well as his mailbox post. All items he had painted using a combination of alcohol, ignorance, and German technology.

It's true, the car didn't look as grand as it once did, but it still ran like the day he bought it. The top still went up and down, even though Dan hadn't had it up for quite some time. He loved riding along with the salt air blowing in his face, and through the slightly receding hairline his father had given him as an unwanted birthday gift. It was the gift that kept on giving every year, just a little more and more.

Coast pulled off the road and into the parking lot of Red's. Dan didn't love too many things, as a matter of fact, he was a take-no-prisoners critic at heart. But he loved Red's. Red's was one of those island bar and grills like you see in a movie that takes place on some unnamed island in the Bahamas or the Virgin Islands. Too clichéd to be real, yet Dan thanked his lucky stars that it was.

Red's overlooked the water. The floor was made of wooden planks whose sticky surface of spilled booze, beer, and soda tugged at the soles of the sandals and flip flops that strolled across them nightly. There were bamboo poles that pretended to hold up a fake thatched roof. More bamboo lined the front of the bar, and there were bar stools with bright orange seats. The walls were wainscoting, stained dark, and decorating the walls were neon beer signs that read Land Shark Lager, Red Stripe, and other popular island brands. There were vintage photos of surfers caught in *Endless Summer* poses, and the obligatory autographed picture of Ernest Hemingway. There were a couple of long boards hanging from the ceiling with several bras resting on top, and hanging over the edges. On Tuesday nights if a girl removed her bra and threw it up on the surfboards and got it to stay she got a free drink. Between the two boards was a ceiling fan. There were two bras hanging from the ceiling fan. Those two girls didn't get a free drink, they just lost their bras.

At Red's you felt like at any minute Magnum or McGarrett could walk through the door, or maybe Brian Flanagan and Doug Coughlin would be throwing rum bottles into the air, making you a drink while "Kokomo" played in the back ground. One look at the place and you knew the guy who decorated it was a guy that watched way too much television in the late '70s and all through the '80s. That man was Red.

Red's real name was Jim Baxter. He didn't have red hair, and he didn't have a red face. That was at least three reasons *not* to call him Red, but no one seemed to know the one reason *to* call him Red. The place was sappy and obvious, and that's why Dan loved it. He, too, had watched too much TV in the '70s and '80s. It was places like this that Dan had envisioned when he decided to move here. Places like this, and people like Red. Red was sappy and obvious too.

Red wore nothing but Hawaiian shirts, cargo shorts, and flip flops. His cargo shorts were always a little too short, and his shirt always seemed to be unbuttoned just a little too far. That is assuming that the crease below a larger man's breasts and the spot where his beer belly starts to head in the wrong direction, is too far. Red stood about six two. He had large hands, large feet, and a large head, a Hoss Cartwright of the island set. He was one of those big and powerful guys that were big and powerful for no apparent reason. No exercise, no weightlifting. The kind of guy you wanted backing you when the going got a little too rough.

Red settled here about six years ago, after his divorce. He was a pizza maker from Chicago. He started out with one small pizza joint that was left to him by his grandfather and turned it into four places within six years. Red managed two places, and his wife of eighteen years managed the other two.

Even though Red's father, a banker, never seemed to have any interest in the family business, he made his only son work there summers and evenings after school to teach him about responsibility and a good work ethic.

When Red was seventeen, his grandfather hired a new waitress. She was sixteen, and the most beautiful woman Red had ever seen. Five years and one business degree later he made her his wife. Eighteen years later it was in that same pizza place, on a surprise visit, that Red found the most beautiful woman he had ever seen in his life, in the storage room, bent over a case of Miller Lite. The beer delivery guy was standing behind her with his pants down around his ankles, sweating and grunting out the phrase, "I got a delivery for ya, I got a delivery for ya," over and over again.

Red owned four pizza places before the divorce. After the divorce he owned two. He sold them both and headed for paradise.

"Manos, Seven, and lime, Red," Dan said.

Red shot him a glance and grunted, "You took the last bottle of Manos home with you last night, pal". Red said.

"Whatever's in the well then, Red."

"That was the well, Dan. You'll have to go top shelf for once in your life, and part with that extra buck," Red kidded.

Red poured a drink from a bottle of Baja, then a splash of 7UP, and a slice of lime. Red always made the drinks too strong. Which was good, because Dan always liked his drinks too strong. Dan squeezed the lime into his drink, pitched it to the side, stirred it with the tiny sword, and discarded that and the little straw too. One thing Dan never did was drink his drinks through a tiny straw like drinking was some kind of a game.

Red leaned his meaty forearms on the bar and observed, "You shouldn't have drove home last night, Coast."

"I had to drive, Red," Dan replied. "I could hardly walk."

"That joke will be funny right up to the part where you kill someone."

Dan waved the barb off and quickly changed the subject. "Hey, did a brunette come in here looking for me? About five-five, too much time in a tanning bed, big fake ones, probably hot back during a Poison concert. I told her to be here around three." Red shrugged.

"Didn't see anyone matching that description. Want to see a menu Dan?"

"Did you change it since yesterday?"

"No."

"Then just give me the fish and chips."

Red turned and made his way back to the kitchen with Dan's order.

Dan took a seat on a bar stool and looked around the room. There was no one else at the bar. There was a table of three, mom, dad, a kid. Tourists. There were two tables of two. A young man and a young woman at each. There was a table of one, a man, late fifties. The man quickly looked away when Dan's eyes met his. Dan pretended not to notice as he scanned the room.

Where is she? Dan wondered. *Did she decide she didn't need my help? Did someone decide for her? Is anyone going to fix me another drink?*

Dan got up from his stool and walked around the bar and proceeded to make his own drink. Red returned with his order.

"I don't need your help Dan," Red scowled.

"Sorry, Red, but I could get a drink a lot quicker in rehab."

Out of the corner of Dan's eye he could see that the lone gentleman was still curious, still watching. Dan decided to bring up the woman again, just to see how interested the man was.

"Yeah," Dan began, "she seemed kind of scared, said her boyfriend had disappeared, said she needed my help. Now she doesn't show up. What would you do Red?"

"I don't know. Why are you asking me?"

Dan quickly turned to the man of interest. Their eyes met.

"What would you do?" The man was caught off guard and choked a little on his drink.

"Wwhat?" the man replied.

"I was just wondering what you would do in this situation," Dan asked the man again.

"I don't know what you're talking about, mister," the man returned, dabbing at the dribble of beer on his shirt.

"Oh, I'm sorry," Dan said, "I thought you were listening."

Dan turned back to Red. "Is he leaving?"

"Yeah, in a hurry. What did you do that for?"

"I just hate it when someone can't seem to mind their own business. Did he leave a tip?"

"No, he didn't," Red said shaking his head. "Thanks asshole."

Dan walked out onto Red's front porch. The sun was going down, and a breeze wafted in across the water. There were about twelve cars in the parking lot now.

Let's see, Dan thought, as he started doing the usual math. *Five drinks, divided by two and a half hours, subtract 190 pounds, and multiply that by Saturday evening. I should be fine to drive.* He walked down the steps and across the parking lot.

As Dan walked up to his car, he noticed a piece of paper stuck under the only windshield wiper on his car. It was a note.

Dan,

Sorry I couldn't meet you. I couldn't come in

Come to my hotel. The Atlantic Inn.

Room 706. I'll explain when I see you

Tess

Chapter Five

Dan Coast pulled up to the valet at the Atlantic Inn Hotel. The Atlantic was one of the larger, nicer hotels on the island. The hotel had seven floors. The first six floors had anywhere from nine to eleven rooms per floor. The seventh floor had six rooms, all large suites, and they weren't cheap.

Dan climbed out of his car and threw the keys to a young man in a black jacket. The young man was Dan's paper boy when he first moved to The Keys. Now he had moved up to valet and was enrolled in college. Dan didn't know why it mattered to him what Billy did, but he liked him and he was proud of him.

"Don't scratch it Billy," Dan warned, shaking a fatherly finger at him.

Billy grinned. "Sure thing Mr. Coast,"

"It's Dan, Billy."

"Sure thing… Mr. Coast." Billy repeated.

It was their usual exchange. Dan winked at Billy and walked through the lobby past the front desk on his right and the restaurant and bar on his left. The restaurant and bar were separated by a carpeted walkway that led through a set of large white French doors to the pool. Dan walked straight ahead and into the elevator, turned, and pushed seven. As a tall brunette made her way quickly through the lobby toward him, the elevator doors began to close.

"Hold the doors, please!" she shouted.

Holding an elevator door was not something that came natural to Dan. In most cases he pretended not to notice someone running toward him, arms outstretched toward the narrowing gap. This woman, however, was not someone that could be easily ignored. She ran toward that door like a *Baywatch* lifeguard ran toward a drowning child. Not so much the urgency, but more the slow motion, up and down movement of her two greatest features. Dan would have to make an exception in this case. He quickly thrust his hand between the closing doors to reverse their movement.

"Oh, thank you," she panted, as she stepped onto the elevator, losing her balance, and falling into Coast's arms. "You're a life saver."

Dan carefully gripped the woman below her floatation devices and righted her. "Yeah, that's me, a regular hero."

"That man in the lounge couldn't take a hint," she explained. "As soon as I sat down at the bar he came over and started trying to buy me a drink. I told him I wasn't there for a drink, that I was just there to get something to eat. He sat down next to me and talked through my whole lunch. Then when I said I was heading up to my room, he wanted to walk me to my door. When I saw the elevator doors open, I made a run for it."

"And now here we are," Dan deadpanned.

She smiled. "Yes, here we are."

Dan smiled back. "I guess that guy just isn't as smooth as me, I had you in my arms in the first three seconds, dancing to this great elevator music."

She cocked one flawless eyebrow. "I guess you did. Are you that smooth with all women, or am I special?"

"Well, I do have that effect on most women, but you're still special."

The young woman laughed as the elevator doors slid open on the fifth floor. She stepped out, turned around and looked at Dan with those eyes that tell a guy, *"You wouldn't have to try very hard."*

"See you around," she said. "Maybe next time we can dance a little slower, and a little longer." The doors closed behind her.

She said slower and longer, Dan thought, and chuckled.

The elevator doors slid open again, but this time on the seventh floor. Dan was still smiling as he walked off the elevator, and down the hall. "703…704…705…706."

Dan knocked. The door was ajar. He looked down and noticed a slipper wedged in the door keeping it open, a woman's slipper. He pushed open the door slowly. The lights were on.

"Hello?" Dan called out. "Hello? Is anyone here?"

There was no answer. Dan walked into the bedroom. The TV was on. *I Love Lucy*, the classic chocolates on a conveyor belt episode. The sound was turned down. No one needs sound to recognize that episode. Dan stopped to watch and grinned. Then he remembered why he was there. His eyes went to two suitcases sprawled atop one of the beds, one opened, one closed. He scanned the room. Two queen beds, no clothes in the closet. A doorway into a living area, and a small kitchenette. Dan walked across the room to the window and pulled back the curtains. *Nice view*, he thought. *I wonder if I can see my house from here.* He put the side of his head against the window. *Nope, can't see it.*

Dan walked into the living area. He could see into the kitchenette. There were a few dirty dishes in the sink, an empty bottle of wine, and two wine glasses on the countertop. A half-eaten bag of Munchos lay on the table, open. *Those are gonna get stale.* He walked over, picked up the bag, took out a couple of chips and ate them. He rolled up the bag and laid it back on the table. He went to the refrigerator, opened it, and took out a diet cola. Dan opened it and took a big swig. *Chek-Mat, someone's been to the Winn-Dixie.*

Dan strolled over to the sliding glass door, slid it open, and walked from the living room out on to the balcony. He looked out at the ocean, then down to the pool. A child in the shallow end looked up at Dan and stuck out his tongue. Dan thought about returning the gesture but stepped back out of sight and returned to the bedroom.

The bed with no suitcases had been slept in, but the blankets had been pulled back up. People do that before the maid gets there. That way she won't think you're a slob. The suitcase that was open was empty. Dan opened the second suitcase. *Women's clothes. She mentioned a boyfriend. Where were his clothes?*

Dan turned and walked back toward the door. Opened it, pushed the slipper back to its useful position, and gently left the door as he had found it.

Dan walked up to the reception desk. A small, well kept, almost feminine looking young man stood behind the counter. He was thin, and pale, too pale to live on an island. He wore eye make-up, an aspect that made Dan's gorge rise. He had a thick head of jet black hair, combed into a kind of pompadour that shined like a beached sea lion under the fluorescent lights. The Goth little fella obviously spent a lot of time on his appearance. He was wearing the same uniform as the rest of the staff, tan khaki shorts and a Hawaiian shirt. His shirt was blue, however. The other staff members wore red Hawaiian shirts. Dan had always wondered if this meant that the young man behind the desk were more important.

"Excuse me. I was supposed to meet a friend of mine. The woman in room 706," Dan said. *His eyes aren't pink. Not an albino, must be a vampire.*

"Mrs. Garvey?" the clerk asked. He had a bit of a lisp. Dan was not surprised.

"Yeah, that's it, Tess Garvey," Dan said, acting as though he and the woman were old friends. "I knocked but no one answered the door. Did she leave a message for a Dan Coast, or say what time she would be returning?"

"No, she didn't leave any messages, but I did see her leave with a gentleman about an hour ago."

"With her boyfriend?"

"No, another man. An older gentleman. They must have just had a fight, because he looked very upset, and she looked like she had been crying."

"The older gentleman, had you ever seen him before?" Dan pressed.

"No, never."

"Do you remember when you saw her boyfriend last?"

The young man thought for a moment. "It's been a couple of days. There was a call for him. I sent Hector out to the pool to tell him. He took the call at the table over there. After he hung up he placed another call, a cab I think. He went upstairs and came down a few minutes later. He had changed out of his bathing suit, and he had a suitcase with him. He came over to the desk and asked me if he could get something out of the safe in the back. We have private safes for each room in the back. I said, 'Yes,' and took him to his safe.

When we got back there, he checked his pants pockets and said he must have left the combination upstairs. He wondered if I could open it for him. I told him that I didn't have the combination that they reset after each guest checked out. I was fibbing of course, there is a master key that opens all of the safes. I have the key, but I wasn't going to let him open it. Not without Miss Garvey's permission. The room is in her name, not his. I offered to call Miss Garvey up to the desk so she could let him into the safe. He said, 'No,' and kept arguing with me, saying I must have a key or something. He became angrier and angrier. I told him I was going to call Miss Garvey. That's when he said, 'Just forget it, faggot' and headed toward the door. Do you believe that? Faggot. Who even uses that word anymore? What are we, in junior high? What a horrible man. I remember once in seventh grade, there was this…"

"Horrible man," Dan interrupted. "What happened then?"

"Oh, um, he picked up his bag and walked out the front door. There was a cab waiting for him. He drove off. That was the last time I saw him."

"Did you ever tell Mrs. Garvey about your conversation with her boyfriend?" Dan asked.

"No. It's not like me to talk about someone behind their back. I don't like drama, or gossip for that matter."

Dan bit his tongue. "Uh, yeah, I'm sure you don't. If Mrs. Garvey returns could you tell her Dan Coast was here?"

"I sure can. Do you want to leave your number with me, Mr. Coast?"

Dan smiled quickly. "No, that's okay, but thanks for the help, I owe you one,"

"I'll remember you said that," the young man said with a wink.

Chapter Six

Coast pulled into his driveway. It was starting to rain so he reluctantly put the top up. He quickly walked up his front steps and onto his porch. As he opened the door he was greeted by one of his few friends, Buddy, a mixture of border collie and black lab.

"It's just me, pal, no one important," Dan said.

Buddy put his head down and slowly turned around and headed back to his bed in the corner.

"I know, Buddy, I wish she would walk through the door too."

Buddy was one of the few things that connected Coast to his old life. One of the few things he brought with him when he moved. Buddy, some photographs, some CDs, a few pieces of furniture, and that stupid car. The car he thought he always wanted.

Buddy was one of those spur of the moment decisions two people in love make while on a day trip to Cooperstown.

"Oh my God, look how cute he is," she gushed.

"Yeah, he's cute alright," came his reply. "Cuter than a yard full of shit."

"Come on, let's get him...please?" she begged.

"Alright, but you're carrying the baggie, and picking up the crap when we walk him. Remember, you want a dog, not me. It's your dog, not mine."

Dan could still remember the smile on her face when he agreed. He remembered a lot of smiles, twelve years worth of smiles.

Dan found himself staring at the picture of her on the small table next to Buddy's bed. Buddy seemed to stare at the picture every once in a while too. Dan often wondered if that dog knew just who that was a picture of. He told himself there was no way that dog could know after all this time.

"Yeah, she sure smiled a lot, didn't she boy," Dan said. His voice seemed to echo a little in the lonely space.

Buddy looked up at the picture as though he understood.

Christ, get ahold of yourself, Coast. You're just ascribing human attributes to your mutt like all those other pet nuts.

Dan shook his head, turned and headed toward the bottles on the buffet against the dining room wall under a large mirror.

"I think Scotch tonight, Buddy, what do you think?"

Coast picked up a glass, walked to the fridge and filled it with ice. Walked back to the table and filled the glass with Scotch. He sat down in his chair, turned on the TV, and flipped through the channels. He stopped on an old rerun of *Magnum P.I.*

"Maybe I should have gotten a Ferrari, Buddy. Maybe things would have been different with a red Ferrari."

Dan looked over at Buddy for a response. Buddy wasn't laughing, he had heard them all before.

Chapter Seven

Coast awoke to the familiar, repetitive sound of a screen door banging in the warm morning breeze. *Forgot to latch the door again.* He looked at the clock. Ten thirty.

Buddy was awake, waiting for breakfast in the doorway.

"Hungry? Come on, let's get you something to eat," Dan said, slapping his thigh out of habit.

Dan walked to the kitchen with Buddy close behind. He put the dog's dish up on the counter. He threw in a couple pieces of bread, a raw egg, two slices of cheese, and a few pieces of lunch meat.

"How's that, Buddy? Better than dog food, right?"

Just then Dan felt the vibration of his phone in his pocket. He reached for it.

"Hello? Hey, what's up, Red? Sure I can do that. I gotta jump in the shower and get dressed, Give me about forty minutes."

Dan looked down and massaged the sweet spot between Buddy's ears.

"Well pal, it looks like you're on your own for the day. I gotta get going, I have a big important job to do today. Red's dishwasher called in sick, so it looks like I'm the dish washer for today. Which also means a free meal for me, and Red will probably throw in a steak for you too."

Dan looked at the coffee pot. Empty. He walked to the refrigerator, opened it. He reached in and pulled out a half gallon container of milk. There was a picture of a young man on the carton. Below the picture it read, "Have you seen me?" Dan showed the picture to Buddy, who was finishing up his breakfast.

"You think this could be that annoying woman's boyfriend, Buddy?" The dog said nothing and gulped down the last morsel of pimento loaf.

Dan shook the carton of milk. He shook it just the way his father had always shaken a carton of milk. Every time he shook a carton of milk he thought about his father. Dan didn't know why he was shaking it. Just a habit.

He opened the carton, took a whiff, made that, *holy shit, I'm glad I didn't taste it* face, and threw it in the sink. Then he went to the cupboard, pulled out a box of Pop Tarts, the kind with no frosting, the best kind. There was one Pop Tart in the box. Open. Left over from a time Dan only wanted one, or three. He tasted the breakfast pastry. Stale as a two dollar whore. He threw it in the sink.

"Looks like Red will have to throw in a breakfast too," he sighed.

Chapter Eight

Coast walked through the front door of Red's. "Where's my apron, douche bag?" he said amiably.

Red didn't miss a beat. "Could you not call me a douche bag in front of the customers, Dan? They don't know if you're a real employee or not."

"Whether I'm a real employee or not doesn't stop you from being a douche bag," Dan said, laughing. Quiet laughter came from the few people who had showed up for an early lunch. Dan bowed comically to the small crowd and said, "Thanks folks I'll be here all night."

"Maybe not," said a voice behind him.

Dan turned to see Rick Carver standing in the doorway.

Rick Carver was one of those people that Dan charitably called an acquaintance. Most locals probably thought they were friends, because of the frequency with which they were seen together in the last couple years. The truth was, the only time they spoke was when it related to someone Dan was helping out.

Rick was never too keen on Dan's helpful ways. There was usually a lot of talk about conducting private investigation without a license. Rick didn't like the idea of someone out doing his job just for fun, like it was some kind of hobby. In some weird way though, Rick thought they were good friends, and that was fine with Dan, because Rick was always eager to talk about his job, and that came in handy sometimes.

Rick was the chief of police. In fact, he was the youngest person to have ever held that position in Key West. Rick had lived in this town his whole life. His father was a cop, as was his father before him. His great grandfather, not so much. Rick's great grandfather, Gabe, had lived most of his life on the opposite side of the law.

Gabe Carver was a so-called pirate. A local legend. As much a pirate as there was in the early nineteen hundreds. As much a pirate as you could be, without ever owning your own boat. The reality was, he was just a small time crook that ran booze up and down the East Coast during the early years of Prohibition. He was shot and killed at the not so very old age of fifty-one, loading three cases of rum into a row boat he had stolen earlier that fateful day. Of course, the rum was stolen as well. Stolen from a man Gabe had sold it to a day earlier. Seems two things went wrong for Gabe that day. One, the man wanted his boat back, and two, Gabe wasn't bulletproof.

Like most local legends, however, the story of Gabe Carver grew and grew over the years. Now he was referred to as, Gabe Carver, the Pirate, as great a freebooter as Sir Henry Morgan or Blackbeard. Supposedly.

About twenty years ago the house where Gabe was born was even turned into a museum. It wasn't much of a house, a two room shanty with an outhouse out back. Up until the shack was turned into a local tourist trap, the people next door, who owned it, used it as a shed. That is until the day someone told the owner of the shed the history behind it. From that day forth it was guided tours Thursday through Sunday, from ten in the morning until five in the afternoon. Ten dollars for adults, five bucks for kids, and anyone under five is free.

"What's up, Rick?" Dan asked.

Rick jerked his head toward the door. "Can you step outside with me for a minute, Dan?"

"Sure thing, pal."

In keeping with the tradition of small town Southern sheriffs, Rick fit the caricature of the red faced, overfed lawman who rather fancies himself and his power. Rick turned and walked out onto the front porch, self-importantly putting on his aviator sunglasses, and adjusting his gun belt as he wobbled down the steps and to his patrol car, with Dan following. When Rick got to the car, he opened the door, reached in, and pulled a photograph from the dashboard. He held up the photo of a woman, bloody, and obviously dead.

"Dan, do you recognize this woman?" Rick demanded.

Dan shook himself out of a momentary stupor. "Yeah, I do. What the hell happened?" Dan asked.

"Have you spoken with her recently?"

"Yeah, yesterday morning. She came to my house to see me, but she looked a little better than she does in that photo. What happened to her?" Dan asked again.

"A jogger found her early this morning. He found her lying on the rocks at the end of Smather's Beach. At first, we thought she must have slipped and fallen, hit her head on a rock. But after speaking to the desk clerk where she was staying, we think there might be more to it."

"How did you link her to me?" Dan asked.

"A paper with your name and address was in her pocket along with her I.D." Rick put the photo back on the dashboard and asked, "So what exactly did she come to see you for?"

"She said her boyfriend was missing. Someone gave her my name and told her I might be able to help. The strange thing was, she said she just buried her husband in Miami last week."

"Who gave her your name?"

"I have no idea."

The chief nodded "Well, I put in a couple calls. I'm trying to find next of kin, or someone who should be notified. I guess I better put in a call to Miami P.D. and find out about her dead husband, and this disappearing boyfriend. Why don't you stop by the station later in case I have any more questions, or if you remember anything else she may have said." He paused and added meaningfully, "Maybe you might remember something helpful."

"Yeah, I'll stop by after I get my lunch dishes done," Dan said.

Rick settled his bulk into the front seat of his cruiser. "Ya know Dan, Laura's up in Kendall for a week, I could use a good maid around the house,"

Dan smirked. "I'll keep that in mind, Cannon"

Chapter Nine

Dan finished up the lunch dishes around three thirty, went to the bar, and took his usual seat at the corner.

"My job in the kitchen is done Red," he said. "Now I have some more important work to do here at the bar,"

"Thanks, Dan. I really appreciate the help. That God damn kid, Juan, calls in sick at least once a week," Red groused. "I would fire his sorry ass but I know how bad he needs the money."

"Not a problem, Red, anytime. Now do *your* job and get me a tequila, Seven, and lime," Dan said grinning.

"My job, he says," Red grumbled good naturedly.

"Red, does Don Rayburn ever come in here?"

"Rayburn? Hell no. Last time he started trouble in here I had Mickey throw him out on his ass. I told him I didn't ever want to see him in here again." Red fixed his eyes on Dan. "Why, are you asking about him?"

"Things seem like they're getting pretty bad over to Frank a... I mean over to Bev's. A lot of fighting, a lot of yelling."

"Yeah, I don't know what she sees in that guy. He's nothing but trouble. I don't think he even has a job right now. I know he hasn't had a license in at least four years. I sure miss old Frank."

"Yeah, me too, Red. Me too."

Dan slowly sipped his drink as he thought about Frank, Bev, and Don. He thought about Tess and the disturbing photo of her lifeless body, the disappearing boyfriend, and the older gentleman that escorted her from her hotel. Why did the boyfriend disappear? Who called him? Did Tess fall, or was she pushed, perhaps by the man she left the hotel with? There were answers to all these questions, but where to find them was another question. *What would a real private investigator do?*

"One more Red," Dan said. "And how about a steak with some fries and a side of mayonnaise?"

Red grinned knowingly. "That steak for you or your pooch?"

"Yeah, but it's not my pooch."

"I'll make it two steaks then."

"Good, that God damn dog hates to eat alone."

Chapter Ten

Dan's Porsche pulled up in front of the police station just as Rick Carver was pulling into the parking lot. They walked up the stairs together and through the front door.

"Where were you coming from, Rick?" Dan asked.

"Out at the beach," Carver replied. "I still have a deputy out there looking around. Who knows, maybe something will turn up."

"Did you hear anything from Miami?" Dan asked as he took a chair as the chief settled behind his desk

"Yeah, I did. Seems she didn't bury her husband this week." The chief paused for effect. "She buried an empty box."

"An empty box?" Dan asked.

"Yeah. So the story I got goes like this: Her husband, Tim Garvey, was on his way home late from his office, lived out on Key Biscayne. It was raining pretty heavy. He lost control of his car and drove it off the Rickenbacker Causeway. Almost made it home, he was only a few blocks from his house. His wife was out of town at the time, so no one realized he was missing. A neighbor spotted the broken guard rail the next morning. Later that day a kid fishing pulled up Tim's jacket with his wallet in it. They brought in divers, found the car, but his body was never recovered. His wife returned later that day and got the news."

Dan whistled "That's some story."

"It sure is. Anyway, it took them a couple months to pronounce him dead, so that's why they just had the funeral this week."

At that moment a look of curiosity and revelation lit up Dan's face. That look of the proverbial light bulb flicking on.

I wonder... Dan rose out of his chair and slowly headed for the door.

"Where are you running off to?" Rick asked.

"Just a hunch," Dan called over his shoulder.

Chapter Eleven

Back at Red's it was getting a lot busier. Thursday, Friday, and Saturday were Red's biggest nights. The rest of the week it was mostly Dan and a few regulars, but on the weekends the joint filled up with tourists, spring breakers, and a lot of locals too. The tourists came because it looked just like what they imagined a tiki bar should look like. The spring breakers came because Red didn't ask for I.D. very often. And the locals came because it was a great place to hook up with a drunk spring breaker who didn't get asked for I.D. and who would be going home in a few days. There was always live music on Saturday nights usually a reggae band or a guy singing Buffett and Chesney songs. Thursday and Friday were karaoke nights. Tourists loved singing karaoke. It's always a lot easier to make an ass out of yourself when no one knows you.

Dan walked through the front door and inched toward the bar, carefully maneuvering between one drunken spring breaker after another. Dan knew Red needed the business, but at the same time he was perturbed that the bar was so full. As he expertly sidestepped a stumbling coed, his shoulder clipped the drink of a young, buzzed up jock. The kid spilled his drink on Dan's shirt. Dan ignored it and kept on walking.

"God-damn college kids," he said under his breath.

"What did you say?" said the college kid, whose ears must have been as well toned as his chest, shoulders, and biceps. He stuck out his FSU-emblazoned chest toward Dan and leaned forward onto the balls of his feet to give the illusion of being taller. This move had worked in grade school to extract the lunch money of the nerds and he was still using it today. You can't teach an *ignorant* dog new tricks.

"Nothing, tough guy. Just settle down," Dan replied.

Dan put his hands up and tried to sidestep toward the bar to avoid any further confrontation with the young man.

"How would you like me to kick your ass, old man?" the kid returned.

"Lick my what?" Dan said, grinning.

"One more word, asshole, and you're going down."

"Like I did on your mother last night, Sport?"

"That's it, old man," Sport said while swinging his right fist at Dan's head. Dan ducked and came up with a hard right to the lower rib cage, then a left to the same spot on the opposite side, then a quick right to the jaw. The young man's head snapped back, and he stumbled backward to the floor. Looking up at Dan with a look of total surprise, he started to say something. Dan interrupted.

"Listen, Sport," Dan said. His brow was low. His eyes were focused on the young man. His finger was six inches from the boy's nose. "I know there's things you think you should say at this point to impress your friends, but if I were you I would keep my mouth shut before I shut it for you... for good. Right now you're sitting on a bar floor, a little embarrassed because an old man put you there. But just think how embarrassed you're gonna be when you're sitting in the hospital because of that same old man. So just keep your mouth shut. You got it, Sport?"

Sport nodded.

Dan hoped the young man would comply. He was already out of breath from the quick exchange and knew he would never withstand another. Dan knew he was too old for this, but hoped that Sport didn't know. The boy took Dan's advice. He stood up, and walked back to the bar quietly, while wiping the small trail of blood leading from his lower lip. When the young man got back to the bar a friend of his handed him a new drink. His friends laughed. Sport did not. Dan turned and made his way to the other end of the bar. There was a drink waiting for him.

Cindy, the bartender, had Dan's drink on the bar seconds after he walked through the door. The ice had melted a little too much by now, and the drink tasted more like water than tequila. She hadn't expected Dan's little detour down, *trying to prove you're not old* street.

Cindy was a spring breaker once. She came down with a group of friends, including her boyfriend, from Loyola University in Chicago. Her classmates were from various parts of the country, but Cindy was from Highland Park, a suburb of Chicago. Daddy had wanted to keep Cindy close to home. She had traveled all over the world on vacations, but never without her family. When she was twenty, her father, Frank Leonard, finally agreed to let her go on spring break to the Keys with her friends. Her friends all went home at the end of the week. Cindy stayed. That was three years ago. Her father flew down immediately to see what, or who had corrupted his innocent little princess. When he got here, he discovered it was a who. The who was Derrick White, a local surfer slash scuba instructor slash maintenance man slash mechanic. Daddy was really shocked when he discovered Derrick was white in name only. Holy crap, what would his cronies at the country club think? Frank voiced several reasons why his daughter shouldn't be with someone like Derrick, but everyone knew the real reason. Frank was a bigot. Dan didn't like bigots.

Of course Frank spent three days trying to convince her to come home, but it's hard to talk a twenty-year-old girl out of her freedom. It's also hard to convince one that she's not in love.

Various threats of disownment proving ineffectual, Frank left without her at the end of the week. Soon after Frank returned to Chicago a check started coming to Cindy once a month from Mother. Six weeks later Frank and his wife bought a vacation home in Key West so a few times a year he could come down and make sure his little princess was alright.

Cindy was slowly shaking her head and grinning when Dan walked up to the bar.

"What the hell was that all about?" she asked.

"Ya know, I don't mind being called *old man*, I just don't like it when it's coming from some douche in a wife-beater with his hat on crooked and his pants two sizes too big. Anyway forty-three isn't that old."

"Well, you are old enough to be his father. And mine too for that matter," she said, laughing. Dan was old enough to be Cindy's father, and had somehow involuntarily taken over the role in some way. Frank Leonard had met Dan at the bar on one of his first visits to the Keys. They talked for a long time the night before Frank went home on one of those visits. It didn't take them long to reach the conclusion that they were each not the other's type of person. They didn't even seem to like each other that much, but yet somehow formed some weird bond of mutual respect. As Frank got up from his bar stool that night, he looked Dan in the eye, pointed his finger at him, and said, "Don't let anything happen to my little girl, Coast...ok?" Dan always remembered the look in Frank's eye that made him agree to the request. He also remembered his first thought after Frank left the bar: *How did that just happen?*

"If I were that punk's father, I would have taught him how to wear a hat," Dan said, still stewing over the earlier incident. "And I would have made him wear a belt."

Dan quickly downed his drink and put the glass on the bar and slid it forward. Cindy knew not to ask if he wanted another, just to make it.

"Is Red in the kitchen?" Dan asked.

"Yeah, he's back there somewhere," Cindy said.

Dan walked behind the bar and through the kitchen door.

"What's up, Jock?" Dan called to the hulking figure at the grill. He always reminded Dan of Lou Ferrigno, and painted green he could have passed for a very flabby version of the actor's most famous role.

"Hey, Dan," Jock said. The butt of his small cigar dangling from his mouth spilled its last ash onto the grill.

"Where's Red?"

Jock waved a leg-sized arm sporting one of Ed Hardy's naked geisha tattoos and said, "In his office."

A year or so ago Dan found out the hard way not to just walk into Red's office on a Saturday night unannounced. Red wasn't the best looking overweight, balding, hairy backed, divorced, forty-nine-year-old man around, but he did have a certain way with the ladies. That is, when the ladies were about twenty-one years old, a little tipsy, a little pudgy, and easily influenced by an older, slightly wealthy man who could provide them with free drinks for the week. So on occasion Red was known to take a young co-ed on a date across his desk, and Dan didn't want to see that horror show again. That scene should only be viewed on the National Geographic Channel, by those with a strong stomach.

Dan knocked.

"Red? It's Dan," he said, carefully peeking around the door.

"Yeah, come in."

Dan opened the door the rest of the way and walked in cautiously.

"You alone?" Dan asked.

"One time Dan, that happened one time," Red responded irritably.

Dan laughed.

Red was sitting behind his desk. Today's Hawaiian shirt was unbuttoned, and a cruise missile-sized cigar was hanging from the corner of his mouth. Red's office was small, and one stogie easily filled the room with smoke. The desk in the room was much too large for the office; it was cluttered with papers in no apparent order. There was a computer monitor and a large orange ashtray that could double as a life raft. Red took a puff on the cigar and placed it in the ashtray, "You want one?" he asked as he leaned back in the chair and clasped his fingers behind his head.

"Sure," Dan answered. He reached toward Red's humidor, opened it and pulled out a cigar.

"What's up, Pal?" Red asked.

Dan picked up Red's cutter, clipped the end of the cigar and then rolled the tip in his mouth to moisten the end. "Hey, Red, remember that guy that was in here yesterday?" Dan lit the cigar, took two drags and blew the smoke into the air. "He was sitting at the table by himself," he added.

"You mean the non-tipper? Yeah, what about him?" Red picked his own cigar up and took a puff.

"Do you think I could go through your security tape from yesterday and see if I could get a good shot of him and print it out?"

"If it was 1970 you could look at the tape," Red said sarcastically, "but today it's digital. It's all right here on my PC, that's personal computer for the electronically challenged." Red's sarcasm was obvious. He knew Dan didn't even own a computer and hadn't got his first cell phone until a year ago. "Just punch in yesterday's date and hit play. Pause it when you get a good shot of him, hit create photo, then hit print photo. A monkey could do it, but if you need help, just yell." Red put his cigar out in the ash tray and stood up to let Dan have the chair.

"Thanks, you're a great teacher," Dan said.

Red left the office and Dan sat down behind the desk and started watching. He fast forwarded to the time he thought the man was in the bar. He watched the screen for about Ten minutes.

There you are, Dan thought as he spotted the man he was looking for.

Dan printed the photo as per Red's tutorial, stuck it in his front pocket and back to the bar he went. His drink was waiting.

"Thanks, Cindy," Dan said, grabbing the lime from his drink and squeezing it into his glass.

He scanned the room to make sure Sport wasn't around, ready to exact some kind of collegiate revenge, just to impress his buddies, but he was nowhere in sight. At the end of the bar though, he did see a familiar face, the brunette from the elevator at the Atlantic Inn. She had already spotted Dan, and slightly lifted her glass toward him. Dan did the same and smiled.

As he made his way toward her along the crowded bar, she did the same. They met somewhere near the half-way point, this told Dan she was just as eager to be with him, as he was to be with her.

"I guess you were right," Dan said.

"Right about what?" she replied coyly.

"Seeing me around."

"I guess so."

"What are you drinking?"

"Malibu and pineapple."

Dan turned toward the bartender.

"Cindy, can I get another Malibu and pineapple here, and another drink for me too, please?"

Cindy quickly made the drinks and slid them across the bar to Dan. He took one and sipped from it, handing the brunette the other.

"What, you don't pay for drinks here?" she asked.

Dan shrugged. "I wash dishes here sometimes, the job comes with free drinks,"

"So, you're a dishwasher. That's impressive," she said, grinning.

"Yeah…it gets the panties off the ladies."

"So you're not staying at the Atlantic Inn?"

"No, I was at the Atlantic visiting a friend. I live here on the island. I have a beach house about a mile from here."

Dan saw a light kindle in her eyes.

"Take me there," she said.

Chapter Twelve

Together they walked up his front steps, through the house, and to the kitchen. Dan grabbed four beers from the fridge and motioned for her to follow. They went out the back door, down the gravel path to the two Adirondack chairs next to the fire pit, a few feet from the hammock from which Dan awoke this same morning. The bottle of Dos Manos still lay under the hammock. It was dark, but with the clear sky and the moon's brightness the ocean could still be seen. The calming rhythm of its breakers completed the mood.

She sat down first. Dan opened a beer and handed it to her, then opened his own and plopped down in the other chair.

"Pretty nice place for a dish washer," she observed. She stretched out her long bare legs and crossed her feet.

"I pinch pennies," Dan replied. He took a sip of his beer.

"You pinch enough pennies as a dishwasher to pay for a beach house in the Keys, and drive a Porsche? That's pretty good." She grinned and took a sip of her beer. A droplet dripped from the corner of her grin landing in her cleavage. Dan watched as it made its way beneath her shirt. She wiped her chin. Dan hoped he wouldn't have to stand up soon. He had no school books to carry in front of him.

Dan never bragged about his financial situation, or even mentioned it to anyone, if he could help it. Only a handful of people on the island knew about Dan's winnings, and even fewer knew the whole story. Dan mostly kept things to himself. Dan believed that the more things people knew about you, the more things they could use against you later.

"So what brings you to our little group of islands...um..."

"Karen. My name is Karen."

"So what brings you to our little group of islands, Karen?"

"My boss."

"Your boss?"

"He owns and operates golf courses all over the country. He had some business to take care of at the golf club here on Key West. He brought me down here with him under the guise of," she made quotation marks in the air with her fingers, "'showing me the ropes.' He's spent the last two days trying to get in my pants."

"So I'm guessing you didn't have any interest in seeing his rope."

"No," she replied, laughing, "I didn't."

Dan built a small fire as they chatted and drank their beers. Dan eventually told Karen that he wasn't really a dishwasher, and without giving her too much information, just told her he was retired. She told him stories about her job and her perverted boss, and how this trip was probably the straw that broke the camel's back. She was fed up with her boss's advances and would probably turn in her notice when she got home. Where home was, she never mentioned, and Dan failed to ask.

"It's getting pretty late," Dan said. "How about if I take you in and show you the rope?"

Karen smiled. "My thoughts exactly."

Chapter Thirteen

"Let me take the Porsche," Alex said, giggling. "I want them to see how wealthy I am."

"Take the Prius. After all you had to have a *Prius*. Dan pronounced the word as though he was munching a turd. I said, 'Get a nice sports car.' you said something about 'the environment and carbon footsteps or something.'"

"It's carbon *footprints*, and the Prius doesn't send the same message," she replied.

"What message *are* you trying to send?" he said with a grin.

"The old *thanks for the going away party, but I never liked most of you anyway* message."

"Well, I'm trying to send you a message. The old *I don't want that God damn dog in my car* message. Besides, I thought they were your friends."

Alex waved her hand in the air. "Two or three of them were my friends. The rest of them I had to put up with just because I worked with them."

"Well, you've just turned into one stuck up little rich girl haven't you," Dan laughed.

"Come on, Buddy, it looks like Daddy won't be letting us use the Porsche today. We'll just have to take my car," Alex said as she climbed into the Prius and drove away.

*****

Dan awoke suddenly to the sound of squealing tires, but there was no sound, it was only a dream. It was the same squealing tires that ended the majority of Dan's dreams. He lay there for a few minutes, beads of sweat on his brow, staring at the ceiling through the hypnotic spinning of the ceiling fan's palm leaf-shaped blade. No matter how many times that dream played over and over again, he could never get used to it. The squealing tires, the crash of twisting metal. Dan wasn't there to witness the accident, but his brain had no problem filling in the gaps.

Dan turned and looked beside him. Karen was gone. Buddy was lying in her place.

"Why are *you* here dog, why you?" Dan asked.

As he got out of bed, he noticed a note on the nightstand. It simply read:

Dan,

Thanks for a fun evening.

Karen

P.S. Nice rope.

Dan almost felt guilty for being glad she was gone when he awoke. No awkward conversation. No promise of a future call. It was almost as though it had never happened at all. Just the way Dan liked it. Karen wasn't the first, and she probably wouldn't be the last woman Dan would use to fill that quiet void between evening and morning. They were piss poor substitutes for what he had lost. But any night that the emptiness was filled with something other than silence, was a night without memories, as long as he was awake that is.

Dan didn't know at what point during the night Buddy had replaced Karen, nor did he care. He reached over and put his hand on Buddy's head. "Where the hell were you last night, dog? You haven't been around much the last few days. You got a new girlfriend or just getting bored with me?"

Buddy sighed and turned his head.

"Man's best friend my ass."

Dan bent over and picked his pants up off the floor, searched the pockets for his cell phone and made a call.

"Hey, Rick, it's Dan. You said Garvey was on his way home from his office. What did he do for a living?"

"He was in real estate. Him and his partner had a company called... Hold on, I got it here somewhere... Here it is, R&G Realty."

"What was the partner's name?" Dan asked.

"Owen Reeves."

Dan wrote "Owen Reeves" and "R&G Realty" on a small piece of paper and stuck it in his pocket along with the photo from last night. He thanked Rick, hung up the phone and placed it back in his pocket.

"I'm gonna take a little trip up to Miami, Buddy. Cindy will stop by and check on you."

Dan went to his bedroom and grabbed a small backpack out of the closet, threw in a pair of pants, socks, underwear, and a couple of t-shirts. After a quick shower, he said a quick farewell to Buddy.

"Later, dog. Take care of the place."

The sleeping dog didn't bat an eye.

"Yeah, I'll miss you too."

Chapter Fourteen

Dan drove along Seaside Way until he came to a small billboard that read,

"Island Adventures"

"Land-Sea-Air"

Island Adventures was owned and operated by Phil Lambert and his wife April. Phil and April were high school sweethearts from Sallisaw, Oklahoma. Phil was the high school quarterback, and April was head cheerleader. They were the homecoming king and queen their senior year, as well as prom king and queen. Phil had been scouted by several colleges, and would have had a free ride, maybe even a spot on an NFL team. April's brains, and grades, along with her father's money, would have let her follow Phil to any college he went to. Much to the dismay of both of their parents, Phil and April had different plans.

Three days after graduation Phil left for basic Navy training and returned eight weeks later on leave to marry April.

They were stationed in Norfolk, Virginia, for six years, Guam for four years, and San Diego for the next ten. Phil and April had always planned to do twenty years and retire from the military to an island somewhere, and that's just what they did. Like a lot of couples, Phil and April were plan makers and goal setters. Unlike most people, however, they followed their plans, and set their goals. The only goals in their life that weren't set as of yet were children and retirement.

They were both thirty-nine years old when they came to the Keys. They were retired for about two weeks when Phil decided to answer the classified ad he saw in the local paper. "Help wanted," it read, "must know your way around boats, planes, and bicycles."

Phil showed up at Bucks Island Adventures later that day with the ad in hand. Phil admitted he didn't know much about planes or bicycles, but he knew quite a lot about boats. Phil and Buck hit it off right away and Phil was hired on the spot. He spent the next six years working on boats and jet skis and learning all there was to know about sea planes and bicycles. He took flying lessons in Miami two days a week and got his pilot's license. Four years ago Buck retired and sold Island Adventures to Phil and April.

Dan pulled up to the office, a one story steel pole barn, and parked. The white shed roof, sloped to the back of the building, and the walls were hunter green. There was a glass door in the middle of the front wall, with a large window on either side. The office sat next to the hangar, built in the same style as the office and the same color. The only difference in the two buildings was that the hangar was twice as high, about twenty feet, and three times as wide, about sixty feet. The hangar could house two small planes, one in each bay, but the second bay was mostly used to store jet skis, kayaks, and bicycles.

Dan pulled open the door and walked in. Seated at the desk directly in front of the door was April, working on a computer and doing paperwork. Standing to her left, with his back to the door, was Phil, pulling papers from a battered four drawer file cabinet.

Looking at April, a petite five foot, three inch woman with light brown hair cut in a bob it was easy to see the prom queen and the cheerleader that she once was. However, it took quite a good imagination to see the ex-quarterback, and military man in Mr. Lambert. With his graying, thinning hair, and his post military pot belly, he looked at least ten years older than his wife. Even though they were both fifty years old, Phil loved to fib just a little bit and tell others that he was fifty-six and his wife was forty-two. He thought it made him look like a stud.

"Phil, are you too busy to fly me up to Miami?" Dan asked.

"When did you want to go?"

"Now, I was hoping."

Phil eased the file drawer closed with a squeak. "Thanks for letting me know ahead of time. You're lucky it's Sunday."

He pushed a button on the phone and spoke into the speaker. "Derrick, can you gas up the plane for me and start the pre-flight?"

A voice came back, "Sure thing, Chief."

"I can bring you up today, but we gotta leave right now and you're going to have to spend the night in Miami," Phil informed Dan. "I have to turn right around and head back here. I have a charter later this evening. Got three fisherman I'll be bringing up to Miami tomorrow morning around nine. You can get a ride back then."

"That's fine," Dan said, holding up the small backpack. "I packed a few things just in case I had to stay the night."

Dan and Phil walked together out to the plane. Phil's plane was a 1966 DHC-2 Beaver that Buck had bought from an old Army pilot in 1983. Phil had it completely restored to showroom perfection in 2007. On the tail of the plane he had commissioned a painting of a grinning beaver in the middle of a bull's eye giving the thumbs up. Underneath the beaver was printed the title, *"The Happy Beaver."*

"All set, Chief," Derrick said.

Phil smacked him on the back. "Thanks, Derrick."

"Hey, Derrick, can you ask Cindy to stop by and feed Buddy for me tonight?" Dan asked.

Derrick grinned. "I sure will Boss,"

Derrick always called people things like Boss, Champ, Chief, or Big Guy. He was always smiling and always seemed to be happy, and he went out of his way to make those around him feel the same way. He was of average height, thin and wiry, his tight white T-shirts showed off his compactly muscular body with almost no body fat. Derrick was stronger than most men twice his size, a fact he had reluctantly proven once or twice when drunken rubes had doubted his manliness.

Derrick White was smart. He seemed to remember anything he ever heard and could recite it back to you word for word. He was one of those rare individuals that could sit down and have a conversation with a homeless man just as easily as he could with the President of the United States. He would treat each no better than the other and seemed to know all about the specialties of both. If anyone ever had a problem with Derrick, it was surely their problem, and not his. He was always on an even keel and enjoyed the Keys lifestyle to the fullest.

As Dan and Phil got on the plane, Dan commented, "This is the second happy beaver I've climbed aboard in the last twelve hours."

Phil groaned. "You should write this shit down, Dan, maybe there's an open mic night at the Comedy Club."

Chapter Fifteen

Dan was startled awake by a bit of turbulence. He turned to Phil in the seat next to him.

"How long was I out?" He asked.

"Not long, probably about fifteen minutes or so," Phil grunted. "Turn on the radio if you want, we should be able to pick up Miami by now. We're about fifteen or twenty minutes out. Strong headwind the whole way."

Dan reached forward and turned the radio knob and adjusted the tuner to find a station. The radio was the only thing on the plane Dan knew how to work, and that was only because it was just an old car radio Derrick had installed one day when he was bored. He turned the knob slowly…*static…static*… "Mangos and Marley you know, fit me like a glove. Sixth gear with nowhere to steer when enough is enough." Dan sat back in his seat. Beach music, Dan loved beach music.

Luckily, so did Phil. They both thought anyone who didn't love it must be nuts. They sang along together, "it's guitars and tiki bars, and a whole lotta love."

"Is it just me, or does this song make you want a drink?" Dan asked, interrupting the Kenny Chesney sing along.

"It's not just you, friend, I would have one with you when we get there, but I gotta turn right around and head back. I got two jet skis down, and Derrick can't figure out what's wrong with them."

"That's ok," Dan replied, "I'm sure I can find someone to have a drink with."

"Hey," Phil said, "you never told me why you were headed up here anyway."

"Some woman came to see me the other day, seems she had misplaced her boyfriend, and wanted me to help her find him."

"Garvey!" Phil exclaimed. "Yeah, I gave her your name."

"So it was you," Dan said.

"Yeah, her and her boyfriend rented jet skis from me last Tuesday. She seemed like a nice girl, the boyfriend was a little odd. Jeff, his name was."

"How do you mean, odd?" Dan asked.

"Well, she talked quite a bit, real friendly, but he kept interrupting her, cutting her off, like he thought she was gonna say something she shouldn't. Real nervous, he was."

"When did you give her my name?" Dan asked.

"It was… Thursday night. She came back to the store around seven, we were closing up. She was pretty upset. She said we were the only people on the island she knew and didn't know where else to go. April and me gave her a ride back to our place. That's when she told us about the missing boyfriend, and the dead husband. That girl had her problems alright. She wondered if there was anyone on the island that could show her around, maybe help her look for him. I asked her why she hadn't called the police. She said she would rather the police weren't involved. That's when I gave her your name."

"Thanks for that," Dan said, "I owe ya one."

"Were you able to help her?" Phil asked.

"No, I didn't help her, but all of her problems have been solved."

"How's that?"

"She's dead."

Phil turned to look at Dan. "Dead…how?"

"Her head made a sudden stop against a rock. They found her at the edge of Smather's Beach."

"So let me guess, Dan, you're going to Miami to play Travis McGee."

Phil picked up the mic and started his landing ritual.

"Miami Sea Plane Base, do you copy? Over."

"This is Miami Sea Plane Base, go ahead. Over," came a voice from the radio.

"Miami, this is November 885 November, approaching from the south, requesting permission to land. Over."

"You're all clear for landing. Over."

Phil turned back toward Dan with a big grin. "After all these years I still think that pilot jargon sounds pretty cool."

"After all these years I still think you sound like an a-hole, over," Dan replied.

Chapter Sixteen

"What style of car are you interested in, Mr. Coast, mid-sized, luxury, something sporty?"

Dan stood at the rental counter. A very tan red head stood behind the counter punching her two index fingers against a keyboard. It was obvious by her poke and jab style of typing, she wasn't hired for her secretarial skills. She was about five foot short, maybe twenty-seven years old. One hundred and ten pounds, fifteen pounds of which appeared to be well placed silicone. She wore a little too much make up and looked more like a stripper disguised as a car rental agent. Dan had gotten a good look at the entire package when she came into the room. It was a sure bet she had a gym membership and knew how to use it.

"I think I'm in the mood for something sporty, Ally," Dan said, looking at her name tag.

"Well, we have a 2011 Dodge Charger, it's red. We also have a 2012 Corvette convertible, silver."

"I think I'll take the Vette," Dan replied. "I'm feeling a midlife crisis coming on."

If she appreciated the jest or even knew what a midlife crisis was she didn't show it. "Okay, Mr. Coast I just need to see your driver's license and a credit card," Ally said.

Dan handed her what she had asked for and signed his name where she had pointed. He only half paid attention as she handed his receipt with a business card stapled to it. He thanked her and headed toward the door.

"Oh, and Dan," Ally called out.

Dan turned back towards her. "Yes, Ally?"

"If you're still in the mood for something sporty later, I get done here around seven. My cell number is on the back of the business card."

"I'll keep that in mind, Ally," Dan said with a grin, as he turned and walked out the door.

He climbed into the silver Corvette that had pulled around for him, adjusted the seat and rear-view mirror, pulled out his cell phone and dialed 411.

"City and state please," the voice on the other end said.

"Miami, Florida."

"Listing?"

"I need an address and phone number for an Owen Reeves, and also for an R&G Realty."

"One moment, please."

When Dan had gotten the information he requested, he turned on the radio, and quickly tuned it to channel 24. Dan loved satellite radio, and for him it was either channel 24 or 25, but usually 24.

Ahh, Dan thought, *the soothing sounds of Mr. Bob Marley.*

He pulled out of the parking lot and headed toward the address the operator had given him for R&G Realty. Reeves' and Garvey's real estate office was only a ten minute drive from the car rental place.

Dan parked the car across the street and walked toward the building. The sign on the post out front said R&G Realty. *This is it alright*, Dan thought, but he could already see the sign on the front door. "Moved to a new location," it read.

The move must have been recent, Dan reasoned, *if the address was still listed here.*

He tried both handles. "Locked," he said to no one in particular.

As Dan turned back to return to the car, the door opened. A large beefy, red-faced man in coveralls carrying an office chair came through the door, his T-shirt soaked through from the day's work.

"Excuse me," Dan said, "can you tell me where they moved to? The sign doesn't say."

"I have no idea," the man grunted.

Dan persisted. "Do you work in the building?"

"No," the man said, pointing at the panel truck in the parking lot, "I work for Jenkins Office Rental. I'm just picking up the last few things. I heard they went out of business though. Money troubles or something."

"Thanks," Dan said, and headed back to the car.

He opened the car door, but before sitting down he reached into his pocket and pulled out a few pieces of paper, and the photo he had printed in Red's office. Dan didn't carry a brief case or even a file folder. He considered his pants pockets the only file cabinet he needed.

As he sat down, he placed the papers on the passenger seat, and pulled out his cell phone. When he found the paper with Owen Reeves' number on it he dialed.

"Hello?" a woman's voice came from the other end.

"Hello, ma'am, my name is Dan Coast. I'm trying to reach Owen Reeves. I'm returning his call."

"What is this pertaining to, may I ask?" the woman inquired.

"I'm not sure, he's been trying to reach me for a couple of days. I guess you could say we've been playing a little game of phone tag," Dan lied to the woman.

"One moment please," the woman said.

I can't believe that worked, Dan thought.

After a few moments a man's voice came over the phone. "Yes? This is Owen Reeves. Who is this?"

"My name is Dan Coast, Mr. Reeves. I need to ask you a few questions about your old partner, Tim Garvey."

"Listen carefully," the man said. "Don't call here again don't try to contact me again, or I'll call the police. Whatever Tim got himself into has nothing to do with me. I don't owe you anything. He's dead, it's over. One more call and I swear I…."

"Listen Reeves," Dan interrupted. "I don't know who you think I am, but I just want to ask you a few questions. Garvey's wife came to see me a few days ago, asking for my help. The next day she turns up dead. Now, you and I are gonna meet one way or another. I can come to your house, or we can meet somewhere. You choose. But it's gonna happen."

"Tess is dead... how?" Reeves asked. His voice was softer, tinged with sadness.

"What's it gonna be, Reeves?" Dan asked.

"Don't come here, please. I'll meet you somewhere. There's a bar on Second Avenue. Blue Moon, it's called. It's only a few minutes from my house. I'll meet you there at four."

"I'll see you at four then," Dan said. He tapped *end call* and slid his phone back in his pocket. He looked at his wrist. No watch. He rolled his eyes and reached back in his pocket to check the time on his cell phone. Twelve-fifty.

That gave Dan about two hours to kill, and he was getting hungry. He started scrolling through local restaurants on the GPS. Suddenly his mouth began to water. Ahh that's the one, and only ten minutes away. *I wonder if they're taking into consideration that this is a Corvette, and I'm really hungry. I say six minutes.* Dan gunned it, spinning the tires, and fishtailed down the street.

Chapter Seventeen

Dan drove slowly down Biscayne Boulevard looking for the restaurant he had chosen from the long list.

"There it is, Barney's Barbecue Heaven," Dan said aloud. "Now that's my kind of place."

He parked in a lot around the corner and walked to Barney's.

Dan waited at the door, obeying the sign that read, "Please wait to be seated."

"How are you today, sir?" asked the hostess, a doughy woman in her fifties, as she walked toward Dan.

"Wonderful," Dan responded. "How are you?"

"Couldn't be better myself, honey. Just one?"

"Yes, I'm going it solo today."

"Right this way, sugar."

The hostess showed Dan to his seat and said, "Candy will be your server today, sweetie. She'll be right with you."

Honey, sugar, and sweetie. What, no handsome? Dan thought. "Thanks," He replied. He pulled out his chair and sat.

Dan hated eating alone at a restaurant. It was one thing to sit at a bar and have a drink and something to eat. But it was another thing to sit at a table in a dining room full of people and be the only one sitting alone. He felt as though everyone was staring at him. Every time he sat alone, he could hear his wife's voice in his head: *Look at that guy over there sitting by himself. Who goes to a restaurant by themselves? I could never sit in a restaurant by myself. I would feel like everyone was staring at me.*

Dan looked around the room. *Looks like a barn*, he thought. Rough cut exposed ceiling beams and lumber. A John Deere sign on the wall across from him. The lights were made from old wagon wheels. Country music played from a couple of speakers sitting atop one of the beams from which depression era farm tools and toys hung.

A few moments later a very pretty, young woman walked up to Dan's table. She was dirty blonde, with blue eyes; about thirty-one probably. The few wrinkles around the eyes told Dan she laughed a lot, and probably had a good sense of humor, two things that attracted Dan to a woman. Not to mention her killer butt, nice tan, and the way her legs looked in that short gingham skirt.

"Hi, my name is Candi. I'll"

"With an 'i,' I see" Dan interrupted, while stealing a quick glance at her pert breasts.

"Yes," Candi said, with a shy grin.

"Do you dot the 'I' with a heart when you write your name on the guest checks, Candi?" Dan asked.

Candi shifted her weight and cocked her head, vaguely aware that she may have been being made fun of. "Sometimes. Why?"

"Just wondering," Dan said, smiling. "You were saying…"

"Hi, my name is Candi," she began again, "I'll be your server today. Can I get you something to drink?"

"Why, yes, Candi, I'll have a tequila, Seven, and lime."

"Any certain brand of tequila?"

"Whatever is in the well would be fine."

Candi poised her pencil over her pad. "Are you ready to order, sir? Or do you need more time?"

"Dan, my name is Dan."

"Are you ready to order, Dan?" Candi said, smiling.

"What would you recommend, Candi?"

"The pulled pork sandwich is good."

"I like pulled pork. Like the late, great Lewis Grizzard said, if it ain't pork, it ain't barbecue."

Candi's face was blank. "Lewis who?"

"Never mind. I'll have pulled pork with fries."

"Okay, sir, I mean Dan, I'll put in your order and I'll be right back with your drink,"

Dan couldn't help but stare as Candi spun on her heels and walked back toward the kitchen. Before she got there, she turned around to make sure he was watching. She smiled, and went through the swinging doors, her perfect butt burning itself into Dan's memory.

Wow, who was the genius that decided on the Barney's Barbeque Heaven uniform?

Dan sat and ate his sandwich and drank his drinks. Candi stopped by the table, a few more times than was necessary, to see if everything was okay, or if Dan needed another drink. Dan didn't mind, he enjoyed the company, especially Candi's company. They flirted a little every time she stopped, even starting an ongoing conversation that would pick up where it left off with each visit. He explained that he was in town on business and would be leaving tomorrow. She told him how long she had worked at Barney's, and where she was originally from, the usual things people talk about at a first meeting.

As Dan was leaving Barney's Candi walked up to him, her face flushed. He could tell she was nervous. Dan spoke first.

"Thanks for the date," he said jokingly, "I had a very nice time"

Candi smiled.

"I don't usually do this... but if you would like to have a drink...or something... later, I get done here around seven."

Déjà vu, Dan thought. He could tell this was something she didn't usually do, just by the shaking in her voice and the look in her eyes.

"You could pick me up...or something," She suggested, flashing her baby blues.

Dan quickly weighed his options. *Hot and sporty, or cute, shy, and smiling?* he thought. *Ally was probably a sure thing, but on the other hand, Candi did know he liked his pork pulled,* Dan laughed to himself.

"That would be great," Dan said, "I'll pick you up a little after seven."

Chapter Eighteen

Coast pulled up in front of The Blue Moon. It was 3:45. He wanted to get there before Reeves, and watch him walk in. See how he moved, study his posture. All the things that tell you what type of a guy someone is before knowing them. Dan walked up to the bar.

"What can I get for ya, pal?" the bartender asked.

Dan's answer was almost robotic, he had ordered it so many times, "Tequila, Seven and lime."

The bartender poured Dan's drink and slid it across the bar. Dan looked down at the drink, then back up at the bartender. Something was missing.

"Sorry, pal, fresh out of limes," the bartender apologized

Dan picked up the drink and walked toward a table in the far corner away from the door and sat down facing it. He sipped his drink and waited. As he waited, he looked around the room, studying it and its patrons. The décor was biker chic: derelict Indian and Vincent motorcycles suspended from the ceiling, a couple of metal Sturgis signs failing to cheer up the vomit-colored walls. Most of the customers seemed to be wearing leather jackets, and the ones who weren't wearing jackets revealed heavily tattooed arms. This, and the fact that there were four Harleys parked out front, told Dan that this was not the type of place that would be frequented by a man like Reeves. Which could only mean one thing; Reeves didn't want to see anyone he might know or anyone that might know him.

Three drinks and thirty minutes later, a man walked through the door. Dan knew right away it was Owen Reeves. This man did not belong here, and even looked a little scared to be here. The man was short and bald. Not the shave head balding men opt for these days as a fashion statement. It was the real, undisguised type of bald most men fear. Losing it in the front at first, then the top. Starting with a comb over that fools no one and ending in a small fur horseshoe wrapped around your head. He stood up straight to give the illusion of a taller man, and exuded confidence, a false confidence. The kind that could easily be chipped away by a larger, stronger man, with real confidence. He reminded Dan of a used car dealer who had once sold him a junk car years earlier. This made Dan dislike Reeves even before meeting him.

When the two men's eyes met, Reeves also knew right away that this was the man he had come to meet.

"Coast?" the bald man asked.

"I am," Dan answered.

"I'm Owen Reeves."

"I know," Dan responded with great sarcasm.

Reeves pulled out the chair across from Dan and sat.

"So what's this about, Coast?" Reeves asked.

"Why don't you let me ask the first few questions," *Coast* replied. "Who did you think I was when I called, and what did you mean by, 'Whatever Tim has gotten himself into?'"

"I thought you were one of the two muscles that have been trying to get me to pay off a debt that Tim had with a local loan shark."

"Debt for what?"

Reeves sighed, looked around the room quickly, and began telling a story that he didn't really want to tell.

"Tim started gambling about two years ago. At first it was small, a baseball game here, a basketball game there. He did pretty well too... at first. But then it got to be more and more, and his luck changed. He was losing and losing. He started to bet bigger and bigger, trying to get back to even. The more he bet the more he lost. I tried to get him to get help. He wouldn't listen, he said he had it under control, and that he had stopped, but he hadn't. Money started disappearing.

First petty cash, small amounts. Then payroll checks started bouncing. When I confronted Tim, he spilled his guts. He told me he had gambled away everything. He said he owed a bookie over seventy thousand dollars, and then borrowed the money from a loan shark and paid off the bookie. Then he turned around and built up another fifty thousand in debt with the same bookie. He told me it was at that point when he started dipping into company funds."

"Did his wife know that all of this was going on?" Dan asked.

Reeves shook his head. "No, she found out when I did. She didn't take the news too well. She threatened to leave him again,"

"Again?"

"Yeah, she moved out for a week or so about six months before this all went down."

"I thought you said she didn't know about the gambling until recently," Dan pressed.

"She didn't," Reeves explained, "she was banging some guy that worked at the marina where they kept their boat. One night she told Tim, she had fallen in love with this guy, Jeff something, and she was leaving him. She came back about a week later after talking to her lawyer. Seems their pre-nup was airtight, it said that if there was any infidelity on her part, she got nothing if they divorced. So she came crawling back begging for forgiveness. She may have moved back in with Tim, but everyone knew she was still jumping Jeff. Everyone but Tim. She told him it was over, and he believed her. He believed anything she told him."

"Sounds like a real nice lady," Dan said sarcastically.

"How did she die?" Reeves asked.

"She fell or was pushed. Hit her head on a rock. A local guy found her while he was out running."

"She was a pretty lady."

"A rock upside the head and a night dead on the beach took care of that."

"She didn't deserve that," Reeves said.

"Back to Garvey," Dan said. "When was the last time you saw him?"

"The night he died. We were at the old office, on Eleventh Street, trying to figure a way out of the mess that he had gotten us into. He was trying to convince me not to call the police. He said he had figured out a way to pay me back. All three hundred thousand."

"Did he say how?" Dan asked.

"No, he wouldn't tell me. He said Tess would explain everything to me later. He closed his brief case. Shook my hand and said that he was sorry for everything he had put me through. That was it. He was killed on his way home that night. Tess had him declared dead as soon as she could so she could get the life insurance."

Dan's interest surged. "Life insurance, do you know how much?"

"We had the same policy, eight hundred thousand. The poor bastard was worth more dead than alive."

"The old George Bailey syndrome," Dan put in.

"Who?" Reeves asked.

"Thanks, Reeves," Dan said as he stood up, "you've been a great help. One more thing."

Dan reached into his pocket, pulled out the photograph, and laid it on the table.

"Is this Tim Garvey?" Dan asked bluntly.

"Yeah, that's Tim," Reeves said.

Dan put the photo back in his pocket. "Thanks again, Reeves. You be sure to have a wonderful life."

Chapter Nineteen

Dan pulled onto the MacArthur Causeway and drove toward Miami Beach. When he came to the end, he took a left and proceeded to drive the length of Ocean Drive. As he drove along his thoughts went to Candi. He was looking forward to his date with her. He looked forward to getting to know her better. He looked forward to just being with her. He always enjoyed the company of a female, but this was the first time in a long time that he actually looked forward to it.

As he drove along, he started remembering a past trip to Miami. A trip he took with his wife. His memories of another time began to sabotage the current joy he was feeling, as it seemed they always did. At first the feelings were of loss and sadness, then it turned to anger. Anger toward the things he felt he missed out on. Then anger toward himself, for allowing these feelings for another woman to creep in.

"Damn it!" Dan said as he pounded his hands on the steering wheel.

When he came to the end of Ocean Drive, he turned the car around and headed back. He reached down and turned up the music, so as to drown out the voices and visions in his head. The voices of past conversations. The visions of plans that never unfolded.

Dan headed away from the beach, back on the Macarthur Causeway, the same way he had arrived. As he came to the Biscayne Boulevard exit, he kept right on driving, picked up his phone and dialed the number on the back of the business card he had received from Ally earlier in the day. Ally was a sure thing, and not just a sure thing in the sack. Not having any lasting feelings for her was a sure thing also.

"Hello?" said the soft voice, as though auditioning for an adult sex line. Dan also detected a slight rasp in her voice that told him she was an occasional smoker. He didn't mind the smell of smoke, and even enjoyed a good cigar now and then, but he didn't like the taste of it on a woman's lips and tongue. Like any man, though, the hotter a woman is, the more he can overlook.

"Still getting off at seven?" Dan asked.

"I am," she responded.

Dan arrived moments later at the car rental. Ally was already waiting outside. She was still wearing her uniform that is, if a plaid mini skirt, high heels, white dress shirt and tie counted as a uniform. But, Dan figured, if it's called a uniform on a Catholic school girl, then it must still be a uniform on a twenty-eight-year-old, bleach blonde, fake-titted, car rental employee. She waved as Dan pulled up.

"Nice car," she said with a grin.

"You should see the chick that rented it to me," Dan replied.

"Was she hot?" Ally asked.

"I'd hit it," Dan grinned.

"If you're lucky," she said with a wink. "You're going to have to run me by my apartment. The clothes I brought to work with me weren't really going out clothes. I'll change, and then we can go get a drink or something. Maybe dance a little. Do you like to dance?"

Dan didn't like to dance, but he nodded anyway, and followed the directions she gave to her apartment.

When they arrived Dan followed her up to her second floor apartment. He looked around and quickly realized that this was an apartment way out of her price range but decided not to question it.

"Have a seat. What can I get you to drink?" Ally asked.

"Tequila, Seven, and lime would be great," he replied.

"I've got ginger ale, is that okay with tequila?"

"Sure," Dan shrugged.

Ally made Dan's drink, handed it to him, and went to her bedroom.

Just as she had seen in a million different chick flicks, she left the door part way open while changing. Dan knew the move; he watched a lot of movies too.

Does she think this is her very own move? Does she think she is the only one who has ever done this?

The only problem with the door left open move, is that the guy never knows exactly what it means, or what he should do. Does she want him to look? Is she testing him to see if he can be trusted? Does she want him to be a gentleman? Does she want him not to be a gentleman? All Dan knew is that it was a game, and Dan hated games.

His thoughts instantly went to Candi with an "i." Candi didn't seem like a girl who would play games. He wondered what she was doing. Was she disappointed when he didn't show up? Was it too late? Probably. She probably got done with work, left slower than usual. Maybe even waited out front for a few minutes hoping he would show. Dan was starting to regret his decision that is until Ally walked back through the door.

Holy crap! he thought.

Ally was wearing a skirt even shorter than the last skirt, and heels even higher than the last heels, and a top that didn't leave much to the imagination. What wasn't falling out over the top was almost coming out of the bottom.

"These are going out clothes," she said.

Dan's eyes bugged. *Those are "laying on the floor next to the bed tomorrow morning" clothes.*

"Are you ready?" she asked.

"I'm ready."

When they had driven for a few minutes she leaned over and changed the channel on the radio. Dan hated it when people did that, especially in the middle of a great song.

"You know, we do allow you to change the channels in these rental cars, you don't have to listen to this old man crap," Ally said.

"Old man crap?" Dan responded, "That's James Taylor."

"I know who it is, my dad used to listen to that garbage."

Dan rolled his eyes. *Garbage? Shit, it's going to be a long night.*

She stopped on some crazy rap/ hip hop/ top forty station and Dan cringed. To Dan, most of today's music was no different than fingernails on a chalk board. There was a time when he listened to music that was a little harder, a little faster. Bands like Poison, Metallica, and a lot of other so-called hair bands. He would even put in a Skid Row CD on a quiet night, and sing along with "Youth Gone Wild," if he were feeling nostalgic. These days though, it was more down to earth music. Music that told a story. So yeah, Dan knew it was old man music, but it was far from old man *crap*.

"Yeah, this is better," he said sarcastically.

Dan slowly began to acquire an appreciation for Ally's music once he noticed the way it made her move. It's very distracting for a driver when a gentlemen's club opens up in the passenger seat. Dan was watching and trying to drive at the same time all the while wondering if this is how she could afford such a nice apartment. After all, dancing like this could get a lot of men to pay a lot of bills.

"Where would you like to go for a drink?" she asked.

"I dunno," Dan replied. "Somewhere quiet, where I can see the water."

"I have a better idea," she shouted, as she turned up the radio. "Turn right up here."

They pulled up in front of a big warehouse with the word "Prestige" written on the front in pink neon. The music coming from the building was so loud Dan couldn't hear the music playing on his own radio. There was a freakishly large bodybuilder type standing in front of the roped off door. About seventy people waited in a long line that didn't seem to be moving. Dan looked at the building, and then skeptically from one end of the line to the other.

"Don't worry," Ally assured him, "I know the owner, we can get right in."

"Awesome," Dan replied. "I'll pull up and drop you off, then park down the street."

"Okay," Ally said as she climbed out of the car.

Dan watched as she got out. *Nice ass. Definitely no underwear.*

The ass, and underwear situation were definitely making it tough for Dan to do what he was about to do. As she closed the door, she started to speak.

"Have fun," Dan interrupted her, and drove off.

As the music from Prestige faded behind him, so did the headache Dan had acquired in the last half hour. He reached down and turned the radio back to channel 24, Margaritaville, and sighed a big sigh of relief as Jimmy sang "Coast of Carolina."

As Dan drove along, he once again found himself on Biscayne Boulevard. The Vette nosed closer and closer to Barney's Barbecue Heaven. He was over an hour late. There was no way she was still there, but something told him he should go in anyway, just to make sure. He parked his car in front of the door and got out. He stood on the sidewalk, staring straight ahead, and feeling like a fool. *What am I doing, why am I here?* He turned back toward his car.

"I'm sorry," a voice said from behind. "Did you wait long? I got this table of twelve just before seven. One of those tables that just wouldn't leave. I was hoping you were still here. Were you at the bar?"

Dan quickly turned to see Candi exiting the restaurant.

"No, I…I was, that is, I just got here a little while ago. My meeting took longer than expected. I didn't know if you would still be here."

"Well, I'm still here. I guess it worked out perfect then."

"Yeah, I guess it did."

Candi fussed with her wrinkled gingham skirt and said, "You're gonna have to swing me by my house so I can change. These aren't really going out clothes."

Dan laughed to himself. This date was starting out the same as the last one, but he was pretty sure it wouldn't end the same.

Chapter Twenty

An hour later Dan and Candi sat on the deck of a small bistro overlooking Biscayne Bay. This was the kind of place Dan liked: the kind of place that Ally just didn't get, but the kind of place Candi had suggested.

"Nice place," Dan said, as he sipped his tequila. A tequila that did come with 7Up *and* a slice of lime. The night was perfect so far.

"I thought you might like it, just by the music you were listening to in the car," she said with a grin. "Are you a Buffett fan?"

"Yeah…we…I" Dan stumbled over his words. "I started listening to him about eight years ago."

"Ever been to a show?" Candi asked.

"No, just never got around to it, something always seemed to come up. Someday, I hope. You?"

"Twice," Candi replied. "Once in the Keys, and once at Jones Beach when I was a kid. My dad took me, he was a big Parrot Head. He passed away two years ago. Now sometimes I'll just put on his old Buffett records. It makes me feel closer to him. Like we're still sharing something. If I've had a bad day at work or something, it just seems to calm me."

Dan's voice calmed. "I know exactly what you mean. It's funny how music can take you back in time like that, to a time when things were the way they should always be."

As Candi talked about her job, her family, and her life, Dan found himself lost in her story. He found himself having unusual feelings of wanting to know more about someone, more about her. Something he had not felt in a long time. He knew that would come with a price, the price of her wanting to know more about him. History had wounded Dan, and the scars of those wounds were thick, and hard to penetrate.

"Listen to me going on and on," Candi said. "You've hardly gotten a word in edgewise."

"No, that's fine, keep going," Dan urged her, knowing that once she stopped talking, he would have to start.

Then it happened.

"So, Dan, what's your story? I know you live in the Keys. I know your name. I know you're here on business. So what else? What do you do for a living? What took you to the Keys?" Cindy asked, her barrage of questions.

This was the point where things usually started to get uncomfortable. This was the time when Dan usually threw up the barriers. But not this time. This time there was something different. This time he felt as though this was someone worth telling his story to. Dan paused for a moment, staring into Candi's eyes. He had told this story a few times to close friends, but never to a woman he was interested in, never under these circumstances.

"I don't really do anything for a living," Dan said. "I'm kind of retired."

"Retired? You don't seem old enough."

"It's a long story."

Candy placed her hand on his arm. "I've got all night."

"I was married for eleven years, and my wife passed away in a car accident a few years ago. It wasn't a drunk driver. She was wearing her seat belt; it wasn't anyone else's fault. It was just one of those freak accidents. Her car was the only vehicle involved."

Candi's face showed genuine interest and concern. "What happened?" she asked.

"The cops think her dog jumped on her lap and she lost control of the car. She hit some guard rails. Alex died; the stupid dog lived. She was on her way to a going away party her office was throwing for her."

"Where was she going away to?" Candi asked.

Dan took a sip of his drink. "Well, you see, we lived in New York and used to vacation down south for a week every year. Myrtle Beach. We both loved the sand and ocean. We would joke about someday winning the lottery and moving to the ocean, maybe an island somewhere. Buying a little beach house. Well, one day on my way home from work, I stopped to get gas at a convenience store. When I went in to pay, I bought a lottery ticket. That night our numbers hit. It was one of those stories everyone hates to hear about. I had never played the lottery before. Something just told me to buy that ticket that night.

A few weeks later we went down to the Keys, looked at some property, and bought a small house on the beach. We went back up to New York to say goodbye to friends and family and to get things ready for the move. That's when the accident happened. Two more days and we would have been out of there. A few days after the funeral I threw my shit in the car, rented a U-Haul and moved down alone. Well, not completely alone, the God damn dog came with me. That was almost three years ago."

Candi squeezed his arm. "I'm so sorry."

"Shit happens, right?" Dan said bravely. "Some days the pile is just a little higher than others."

Dan took another sip of his drink and stared out at the water. He could feel a small lump growing in his throat. Always a good time to stop talking. He didn't make eye contact until Candi restarted the conversation.

"So, you said you were here on business, but yet you said you were retired, how does that work?"

"No, I said I was kind of retired."

"What's… kind of retired mean?"

"Funny story actually," Dan began. "A couple years ago, I kind of accidently solved a local murder."

"How do you accidentally solve a murder?" Candi asked, hanging on Dan's every word.

"Well, it all started when this college kid came down to the Keys on spring break with some friends. One night they were all out drinking, he gets separated from his buddies. The kid's wandering the streets, alone and drunk. These two local losers, Trey Bingum and Dusty Rob, come upon the kid. They got tough with him, he got mouthy. Trey and Rob got the kid into an alley and tried to roll him. The kid fought back. One thing lead to another, and two days later some guy was taking out his garbage, and found the kid in a dumpster."

Candi's eyes were as big as dinner plates. "So then, how did you happen to solve the murder?"

"I was just in the right place at the right time. I overheard one of the guys who did it, in a bar one night."

"How do you just happen to overhear someone in a bar confessing to a murder?"

"Well, I went into the bathroom, into a stall. While I was sitting there, these two guys come in. One of them was this Trey Bingum, the other one was another friend of his there to warn him that Dusty Rob was going to the cops to turn him in. He figured the cops would go easy on him if he testified against Trey. Rob said Trey was the one who hit the kid in the head with a pipe. I pulled up my feet so they wouldn't know I was there. I sat there and listened to the whole story. Even their plan to set up Dusty Rob and kill him.

So I went to an acquaintance of mine, who is also the chief of police, with the information. I didn't tell him how I got it of course. The cops went to Dusty, told him what was about to go down, and when. They put a wire on him in exchange for a lighter sentence. Trey and his buddy showed up, babbled off a bunch of incriminating evidence, and the cops busted in and arrested everyone. I got a reward, and a nice write up in the *Citizen.*

"Good thing you didn't tell your friend how you got the information. I can see the headline now, *Crapper Clues Crack Coed Caper.*"

"Very funny." Dan said. "Remember, I told you that in confidence."

"Your secret is safe with me," Candi giggled. "So how did that turn into a part time career?"

"Because of the newspaper write-up people started calling. A few weeks later, this woman comes to me and said she thought her husband was cheating on her and wondered if I could help her. I took a few pictures. She gave them to her attorney. She did well in the divorce. It kind of snowballed from there and now I just help people when they ask me. For a price, of course."

"So you're like Magnum P.I.," Candi said with a grin.

"No, that would be like saying Bob the Builder is like Jesus," Dan said with a laugh. "Besides, you have to have a license to be a private investigator. Me I just help people when they ask."

"Well I think you're as handsome as Tom Selleck," Candi purred.

"How many drinks have you had?" Dan shot back.

They laughed. And kept laughing and talking at the table overlooking the water until the bartender called out *last call*. Dan told her more about his life and Candi told him more about hers. As Candi talked, Dan interjected now and then with his usual wit and one-liners, and Candi would laugh. She seemed to laugh a lot, and Dan liked that. He liked it a helluva lot.

Chapter Twenty-One

Dan awoke the next morning in his hotel room alone. The evening didn't end in the same way it would have if he had hooked up with Ally, the sporty model. There was no clothing thrown about the floor. No moans and groans. There was no nudity, no sweaty bodies grinding together in the throes of passion. No hangover. No ringing ears from the loud dance music. No wondering why she was still here. Just a big stupid grin.

Dan was happy the way things did end, with a kiss at Candi's front door, a hug, and the exchange of phone numbers. It ended the way a first date should end. As far as Dan was concerned, the evening was perfect, and he couldn't have hoped for a better parting.

The alarm clock said seven twenty-one. Coast had about an hour or so to get to Dodge Island to catch his ride home. Phil was one of those people that were always punctual. A leftover obsession from his military days.

Dan knew his biggest problem this morning would be dropping the rental car back off undetected by Ally. He was hoping it was her day off, or possibly she had gotten too drunk to make it to work. Dan knew Ally probably didn't end up going home alone, but that wouldn't stop her from being pissed at the guy who drove off and left her standing at the curb.

All the way to the rental office Dan tried to plan out what he would say if he was confronted by Ally, what excuse he would make up. Should he say he wasn't feeling well? Should he say he parked the car, but lost her in the crowd? Every excuse would surely sound like a lie to a young woman left mid-sentence at the curb side.

So he took the coward's way out, and left the car in the parking lot and had a cab waiting to take him to the seaport. Dan wasn't scared of too many things, but not knowing how a woman was going to react to something stupid that he had done was a fear he always tried to avoid.

Chapter Twenty-Two

Phil was right on time as usual. Dan got on the plane and was home by ten-thirty.

As he pulled into his driveway, he noticed that his front door was standing wide open. He shook his head. *No one under twenty-five knows how to shut a door*. As he walked through the door he called out to Buddy.

"Honey, I'm home."

Buddy sat on his bed, staring at Dan.

"Did you leave the door open, or was it Cindy?" Dan asked Buddy.

Suddenly Dan was startled by movement behind him. As he turned to look, he felt something smash against the side of his head. He stumbled backward. His head felt wet. He touched his head; he looked at his hand; his hand was covered in blood. He blinked and shook his head to try and regain his wits, but it was too late: a fist was connecting with his jaw, and everything flashed white and then went black.

Chapter Twenty-Three

Dan slowly opened his eyes. He was sitting in a chair. Lying next to the chair was a broken tequila bottle.

Good God, he thought, *did I drink that, or did someone hit me in the head with it?* There was blood on his pants that had run down his leg onto the floor. The blood had already dried brown. He could smell the blood. It smelled like your hands after rolling pennies. He could feel that his pants were stuck to the hair on his leg. *Jesus, I didn't know there was that much blood in me.*

He couldn't move his arms or legs. It didn't take him long to realize he was duct taped to the chair. His head hurt badly his vision was blurry. He shook his head; that made it worse and he winced in pain. His hands and feet were numb. *How long have I been tied up?* he wondered. He slowly lifted his head to look around. Buddy was sitting in the exact same place, still staring at Dan.

"Thanks for the heads up, asshole," Dan whispered to the dog. "I suppose you showed him where I keep the duct tape."

He could hear movement coming from his bedroom and someone mumbling to themselves. He also noticed drawers pulled out, and furniture tipped over.

If this was a robbery, they wouldn't still be here, he reasoned *I don't have that much stuff.*

Just then a man emerged from Dan's bedroom. The room was dark. The shades were pulled. Dan had trouble focusing on the man's face.

"So, you're not dead. You must have a pretty thick skull," the stranger said.

"I've been told that," Dan replied. "What are you looking for?"

"I think you know what I'm looking for."

"I think I don't."

The man walked over and slapped Dan on the open wound of his head.

"God dammit!" Dan yelled out.

"I can do that over and over again until you tell me where it is. I know she was here. I followed her. I know she brought it with her."

"Who brought what?" Dan asked again.

The man walked toward Dan, hand raised again, ready to strike.

"Wait! Stop!" Dan shouted, "Listen, you can hit me as many times as you want, I still won't know what you're talking about."

"Tess!" the stranger yelled. "I know she was here, I followed her. She had the suitcase when she got here and she left without it. So it's here somewhere." The man looked around the room and shouted. "Where is it?"

"I told you I…"

He slapped Dan again.

"Shit! Fuck!" Dan hollered. "You better kill me now, you bastard. You're a dead man if I get free."

Just then Dan noticed Rick's patrol car pull up out front. The unknown man saw the look in Dan's eyes, turned toward the window and saw the cop car. He started running toward the back door.

"Rick…Rick!" Dan called out. His voice was hoarse, and it hurt his head to yell.

It was no use, Rick's windows were up and the air conditioner was running. Dan could see through the window as Rick sat in his car, grinning to himself as he texted someone. Dan sat calmly waiting for Rick to finish his virtual conversation. Dan looked toward Buddy.

"Why don't you run out there and get him, God damn flea motel. You wouldn't be worth shit if Timmy fell down the well," Dan said in frustration.

Buddy lay back down on his bed, and Dan laid his head back and sighed out a "Good God!"

After Rick was done with his socializing, he finally came inside the front porch. He immediately saw Dan through the screen door and drew his weapon. He slowly made his way to the doorknob and pulled it open, trying not to make a sound. Dan just sat there blank faced and stared at Rick. Rick entered the room weapon first, slightly crouched.

"Are you gonna shoot me?" Dan asked.

"Is someone here?" Rick whispered, holding his gun in one hand and his cell phone in the other.

"There was, but I think you scared him off with your superb texting abilities, and that scary, stupid grin," Dan replied.

"It was Emily," Rick said, holding up his phone. "She's coming home early. Her sister's driving her nuts, and those little rug rats of hers are…"

"Really Rick, *really*?"

Rick's cheeks glowed red. "Let me call you an ambulance, Dan,"

"And maybe untie me?"

"Oh yeah, that too."

Chapter Twenty-Four

Dan sat on the edge of the examining table as Linda Briddle sewed up the gash on the side of his head.

"I told you tequila would be the death of you, Dan," Linda said, straight faced.

Linda never cracked a smile when delivering her own brand of dry humor. Often times it was difficult to tell if she was kidding, or being dead serious, because her demeanor didn't change in ether instance. Her expression was the same whether telling someone a loved one had passed away or telling a dirty joke. And no one loved hearing or telling a dirty joke more than Doc Briddle.

Linda Briddle was a local. Born and raised in Key West. Graduated from Key West High. Her only time living away from the Keys was her time at Boston University. The good doctor was a big woman, put together more like a man than a woman. She was tall and outweighed Dan by at least thirty pounds. She had hairy arms, and Dan figured she must shave, because sometimes her face was smooth and other times she sported a forest of stubble that would make a lumberjack proud. She never wore make-up. There never seemed to be a man in her life, although Red did tell Dan about a one night stand he had with her when he first came to the island. The story was only told once when Red was very drunk, and never mentioned again. Dan didn't know if the story was true or not.

"That's pretty funny, Doc. It was funny when Rick said it, it was funny when Carl said it in the ambulance on the way here, but I think it's the funniest when you say it."

"It's all in the delivery and timing, Dan." said Linda with her usual poker face. "Listen, I'm gonna want you to spend the night. The X-rays didn't show any skull fractures, but I'd like to keep an eye on you tonight anyway. That was a pretty good shot to the head. You lost a lot of blood, a hit like that could have killed you."

Later, when Dan had settled into his room, Rick stopped by to see how he was doing. He brought a couple magazines, a change of clothes he had picked up from Dan's house, and a greasy paper bag from Red's with two cheese burgers and fries.

"Hey, Dan, how ya doin? Feeling any better?" Rick asked.

Dan motioned for his guest to sit in the bedside chair. "I'm feeling a little better. They got me on some pretty good painkillers. Only thirteen stitches."

"Yeah, I guess it looked worse than it was."

"I know it *felt* worse than it was."

"So, who do you think it was, what do you think they wanted?"

"It wasn't anybody I've ever seen before. I guess it was just a tourist or someone off the beach trying to rob the house. I guess I just came home at the wrong time."

Dan knew he shouldn't be lying to Rick, but he knew he would be telling him the whole story eventually. As soon as Dan himself learned the whole story.

"Besides, the whole thing is kind of blurry. I can't even really remember what he said or what he looked like," Dan lied.

Rick stayed for a while, somehow getting comfortable in a chair that was not built for comfort. Nor was it built for a man of Rick's size. They watched an episode of *The Price is Right*, and each had a cheeseburger and chatted. Rick told Dan about the fence he wanted him to build out front of his house next to the sidewalk. Dan told Rick about the shed he had to build for Phil in exchange for the plane ride into Miami. Halfway through *Rachel Ray*, Rick got up, and said he had to get back to work. Dan thanked him for stopping by.

Now Dan lay alone in his room, except for the nurse that came in every hour to wake him up and see if he was sleeping okay, and to check his vitals. As he drifted in and out of sleep he thought of Tess, and the missing boyfriend. He thought about the dead, but not really dead, husband. He thought about the man who invaded his home, the man he said he was going to kill.

Eventually, though, his thoughts went to Candi. What she might be doing at that moment. Was she thinking about him? Should he call, how long should he wait to call? Would she call if he didn't? A feeling of slight embarrassment came over him as he realized he was having the same thoughts a teenage boy would have about a pretty girl he had just met. A grin came over his face.

"What are you grinning about, Dan? That must be some pretty strong stuff I got you on," Linda said as she walked into the room.

The smile quickly left Dan's face.

"You ever heard of knocking?" he said.

"I don't have to knock, it's my hospital. How ya feeling?"

"Just a little headache. My vision isn't blurry anymore, and that irritating noise in my ears stopped as soon as Rick left the room."

Linda did the usual things: felt his pulse, took his temperature, and blood pressure.

"Everything looks good. I'll be in about nine-ish tomorrow morning. I'll take another look at you and then you can get out of here." She picked up a clipboard that hung at the foot of Dan's bed and reached into her breast pocket and pulled out a rectal thermometer and started to put it to the paper. "Shit! I wonder where I left my pen?"

Dan smiled. "Thanks, Doc."

Chapter Twenty-Five

Rick was at the hospital first thing in the morning to give Dan a ride back to his house. Dan didn't talk much on the way home. His head still hurt, and he was deep in thought. He wondered what he should do next. Where should he start, who should he talk to first?

They pulled up in front of Dan's house.

"There ya go, pal. Just yell if ya need anything," Rick said.

"Thanks Rick. I'll do that," Dan said.

As he walked up his front steps and through the screen door Dan was startled by Cindy, who was on her way out.

"Jesus, Cindy! You scared the crap out of me," Dan yelled.

Cindy put her hand on her own chest. "Sorry, Dan. I guess you're a little bit jumpy after what happened yesterday. Me too. I just came over to feed Buddy. I didn't know what time you would be home today."

"Thanks, I didn't mean to yell at ya. Hey, how did you know what happened to me yesterday?"

"Everyone knows. Phil told Derrick, and Derrick told me. Even your friend stopped by to see if you were home yet, he knew about it too."

"Friend, what friend?" Dan asked.

Cindy bit her lip in thought. "Ya know, he never said his name. He said he was down here from Miami, heard you were in the hospital, and he stopped by to see if you were okay."

"Did you let him in?"

"No, we talked at the door. He offered to come in and help me straighten up, but I said no thanks, I could do it."

"How long ago did he leave?"

"About a half hour ago I guess."

Dan reached into the bag of yesterday's clothes he was carrying, went into the pants pocket, and pulled out the picture of Tim Garvey.

"Is this my friend that was here?" Dan asked.

"Yeah, that's him. He said he would probably stop back by later."

"Cindy, it's probably best if you don't come around for a few days, at least till we get this guy that did this to me. It might not be safe."

"Okay, Dan. Oh, yeah, and Bev and that idiot were fighting all morning. I don't know what she sees in that guy. Frank was so nice; this guy is just a jerk. I thought about calling the cops, but I haven't heard anything from them in a while. Do you think I should go over and see if everything is okay?"

"No, I'll stop over in a bit. Don't you worry about it."

Cindy left and Dan started cleaning up the house where Cindy had left off. After a few minutes he made himself a drink, a double shot of Scotch, no ice. Then he walked over and sat down in his chair, reached for the bag he had brought from the hospital, and pulled out a bottle of pills. He read the label out loud:

"Take one capsule as needed if pain persists. *As needed*? That leaves a lot of room for interpretation, don't ya think?" Dan said as he looked toward Buddy. "By the way, dog, have you seen a suitcase around here? Someone wants it real bad. Now we just have to figure out who wants it, and why."

As usual, there was no response from Buddy. He walked over got a drink from his water dish and returned to his bed for a nap. Dan opened the bottle of pills, poured two into his hand, threw them to the back of his throat, and chased them down with a swig of the Scotch. He laid his head back and drifted off to sleep.

Dan's nap was a short one, however. He was soon startled awake by the creaking of his back door and the slowly applied pressure to the steps that lead to the creaking door. The obvious sounds of someone trying to come in undetected. The same sounds made by a fifteen-year-old kid coming home from their first encounter with alcohol. Dan had made the noise plenty of times as a kid, and heard his sister make these same noises plenty of times. The only thing missing from this entrance would be the direct beeline to the bathroom to drink a cup of mouthwash. Dan sat perfectly still, not wanting to let the intruder know that he had been detected.

"What's up Dan? How ya feeling?" Red called out.

"Holy Christ! What's wrong with you people?" Dan moaned.

"What's wrong?" Red said, entering the living room.

"What's wrong? You scared the hell out of me, that's what's wrong. Someone snuck into my house yesterday and kicked the shit out of me, and now everyone sneaks in to see how I'm doing, and this God damn dog never makes a sound. What ever happened to coming to the front door and knocking?"

"Sorry, I didn't want to disturb you."

"Well, I'm pretty disturbed."

"Are you sleeping?"

"Not now."

"How's your head?"

"It hurts like hell."

Dan got up from his chair, shaking his head, and went to the bar to make Red a drink.

"Rum and Coke, Red?"

"Sure." Dan made Red's drink, handed it to him and motioned for him to follow him outside. On their way out the door Dan bent down and picked up a ball that was lying on the kitchen floor.

"Come on, Buddy," Dan called out.

Buddy got up from his bed and followed Dan and Red down the gravel path, past the chairs, fire pit, and hammock and out onto the beach. When they got to the beach Dan threw the ball into the water. Buddy chased after it.

"So, how's your head Dan?" Red asked.

"You already asked me that. It still hurts a little. They gave me some pretty strong pain pills. That, mixed with the booze, works pretty good."

"Any idea who it was?"

"Yeah, I got a pretty good idea."

"Does it have anything to do with the case you've been working on?"

"It's not a case, Red. It's…more of a hobby."

"Seems like it's turning out to be a pretty dangerous hobby, pal."

"Well, it started out as a missing person. Who knew it would turn into murder, and me getting my head bashed in?"

Buddy brought back the ball a few more times, and Dan kept throwing it down the beach. Dan and Red walked along the beach, and Dan filled Red in on everything, not that he needed or even wanted Red's help at this point. He just wanted someone else to know exactly what was going on in case anything happened to him.

Dan finished his story about the time they got back to the house and walked up to the lawn chairs. Red sat down, and Dan went in to make two more drinks. When he returned with the drinks, he also sat down.

"So, what are ya going to do next Dan?" Red asked.

"There's not much *for* me to do. There are two guys on this island: a boyfriend with a bad temper, and a dead husband. The wife, who is also the girlfriend, is dead, but neither guy seems to want to leave the island. There's something keeping them here, and at least one of them thinks I know what it is, and where it is. My guess is, I don't have to do anything. Eventually these guys are going to come to me. If I get impatient, I'll go to them."

"This is so exciting," Red said. "It sounds like an old episode of *Riptide.*"

"I'm glad I can provide you with such great entertainment, Red.," Dan said shaking his head. "Shit,

I barely remember that show. You could at least compare my beachcombing lifestyle to Magnum P.I."

"There's a reason for that. If I compare this to Riptide, that kind of makes me Cody Allen. If I compare it to Magnum, that will make me Higgins," Red said laughing. "I have to get back to the bar, Dan. Stop in later if you feel up to it. I'll cook us up a couple of nice juicy steaks."

After Red departed, Dan stayed in his chair, put his feet up on the fireplace and sipped his drink. Buddy walked over and laid down beneath Dan's legs.

"I'm going to take a little nap, Buddy," Dan said. "Do you think you could give me a little warning if someone's gonna come up and hit me in the head with a friggin bottle?"

Dan put his head back and closed his eyes. He could hear the wind through the palms, the crashing waves, and the lonesome call of the sea gulls, and Don's mouth from next door. He was bitching about something. Who knew what?

"Jesus Christ!" he said aloud. "Why can't I just get a little peace and quiet?"

Dan stood from his chair and walked with clenched fists toward Bev's. When he got to the back screen door he could hear Don's bellowing voice.

"What are you, stupid?"

"Why, what did I do?" Bev's voice replied, weeping.

"Why what did I do?" Don repeated, mocking Bev. "You think I don't know why you're always at that grocery store? You think I don't see the way he looks at you? You dress like a whore. Why don't you act your age? I know you're screwing him."

"I'm not. I swear, Don. I haven't done anything," Bev sobbed.

"You mean you haven't done anything yet, but you will. Sluts like you *always* do."

Dan stood at the back door listening. He knew he shouldn't, but he didn't want to walk away, and he didn't want to enter. He was surprised to find himself knocking.

"Bev? It's Dan. Is everything okay?" Dan called out through the screen.

"Oh great, it's your knight in shining armor, here to rescue you," Don yelled.

Don walked from the living room to the back door, drink in hand.

"What do you want?" Don asked Dan.

"I want to talk to Bev," Dan said.

"Well, you can talk to me, I'm the man of this house."

Don's speech was slurred. It was obvious he was half in the bag. He was belligerent and wanting to fight. A fight Dan didn't want, but a fight Don didn't want even more, he just wasn't smart enough to know it. Bev had lost one guy and didn't need to see another one get beaten in front of her. Besides, Dan probably couldn't take another hit to the head right about now.

"Everything is okay, Dan. Just leave, please," Bev called out from the other room.

"Are you sure?" Dan replied.

"Yes, please, just go. I'll talk to you later."

"Yeah, she'll talk to you later, Sir Dan Coast," Don said sarcastically, braying like the jackass he was.

Don slammed the door.

Dan went back to his house, made another drink, walked back to his lawn chair, and tried to get some sleep. The fighting had stopped, and all was quiet for now.

But it felt like the calm before the storm.

Chapter Twenty-Six

Dan awoke a few hours later; the sun was down but it was still light out. The breeze had stopped, but it had gotten a little cooler. Buddy had left his post and was a few yards away, digging in the sand.

"Whatcha looking for, Buddy?" Dan asked. "Did ya bury a bone over there or something?"

Buddy ignored Dan, as usual, and kept digging. He was only about four inches below the sand when his paws started scraping across the top of something. He kept scratching as though he was trying to dig right through his find.

Dan yawned and stretched. His back ached from his long snooze in the hard-backed chair. "What do ya got there, pal, an old pirate's treasure?" Dan asked.

Dan got up from his chair and walked over to the shallow resting place of Buddy's unearthed treasure.

He knelt down to help Buddy pull the object from the sand. As Dan reached into the sand, he felt a handle and pulled it. It was a small suitcase, or large briefcase, made of black leather. The masculine look of the case told Dan it had probably belonged to a man. It just wasn't the type of case you would expect to see carried down the street by a woman. Dan wondered who's it was and how long it had been there.

Dan laid it in the sand next to the hole. As he was brushing off the dirt and sand, he noticed an emblem on the side, "R&G Realty," and letters near the handle. "TAG," the letters read.

"Tag?" Dan said to Buddy. "I don't know what the A stands for, but I bet the T and G stands for Tim and Garvey."

"Very good, Mr. Coast," came a fast-approaching voice from behind Dan.

Dan looked to his right. In the sand beside him were two black dress shoes. Not the type you see at a beach house in the Keys. He slowly looked up from the shoes, to the pants, to the shirt, to the face. There he was. The man in the bar. The man in the picture. The dead husband. In his hands was a shovel.

"You're not here to borrow my shovel, are ya?" Dan quipped.

Garvey managed a smirk. "No, I'm not."

"You're not gonna hit me in the head with it, are ya?"

"I don't want to."

154

"Thank God! Where did ya get my shovel from any way?"

Garvey jabbed the blade of the shovel into the sand and leaned on the handle. "It was over there leaning against the tree. I would imagine my wife left it there when she buried my suitcase in your yard…5032."

"5032?" Dan repeated.

"The combination to the briefcase, Coast."

Dan turned back toward the briefcase. To the right of the handle were four small brass wheels, each containing several numbers, Dan slowly turned the wheels to the combination that Garvey had given him. When all four numbers were in their proper order Dan pushed the button beside the numbers. The latch popped open. Dan opened the case. It was empty.

"Empty," Garvey said quietly.

"What were you expecting to find in there?" Dan asked.

"Eight hundred thousand dollars."

Dan looked back up toward Garvey and stuck out his hand. He didn't need Garvey's help to get to his feet, but it was a good way to see just how friendly this meeting would go. Garvey stuck out his hand and helped Dan up. Dan then reached out his hand toward his shovel, Garvey's potential weapon. Garvey handed him the shovel. Dan leaned it against the lawn chair.

"Let's talk, Garvey," Dan said as he motioned toward the house. "We'll go inside. We don't want the wrong person to see you here."

As Garvey sat in the living room, Dan made them each a drink. He slid a dining room chair across the floor and faced it toward Garvey. He handed Garvey his drink and sat down. Buddy lay on his bed, listening intently, as if to pick up on a clue that Dan might miss out on.

"Where do you think the money is, Garvey?" Dan asked.

Garvey took a big swig of his drink, held it in his mouth while twirling the ice in his glass. He swallowed. "I think I might know who has it."

"No, he doesn't. Jeff doesn't have it."

"So you know about Jeff Hinder. How do you know he doesn't have it?"

"Because he came to see me the other day. He's the one that put this lump on my head. I walked in on him tearing my house apart. Now I know what he was looking for, and now I know what your wife meant when she said, 'He wouldn't have left the island without her.' My guess is, he still hasn't left the island, and he's not going to until he gets the money. So this brings me back to my original question. Where do you think the money is, Garvey?"

"I have no idea, Coast," Garvey answered.

Dan stared into Garvey's eyes for a moment. He was telling the truth. He had no idea where it was.

"Your wife must have hidden the money somewhere before she got to my house. She must have kept the suitcase to throw Hinder off the trail. He knew she came here. He must have followed her, then came back later to get the money when he knew I was gone. He must not have known she buried the case, or he would have dug it up himself, and I'm sure he didn't know it was empty." Dan said.

"So the money is somewhere between her hotel, and your back yard. That narrows it down," Garvey said sarcastically.

"Did you kill your wife, Garvey? Did you push her down on the beach?"

"No." Garvey replied simply.

"I didn't think so, but where did you take her when the two of you left her hotel Wednesday evening?"

"You seem to know everything else; I can't believe you don't already know the answer to that."

"Well, I don't, so if you want me to help you get your money back and find Hinder then you might want to just start from the beginning. I already met with Reeves a couple days ago. He filled me in on the gambling, the loan shark, the bookie, your wife's infidelity, and the insurance money. Why don't you just start from there?"

"Reeves is here?" Garvey asked, surprised.

"No, I went to Miami."

"How's he doing?"

"As good as you would think. He's lost his business. His partner stole three hundred thousand dollars from him. I think he'll be okay eventually."

"Yeah, he was always better with money than I was," Garvey said, lowering his head in shame.

"Obviously," Dan stated. "He said something about a plan you had to pay him back…"

"That's why I have to get this money back, Coast," Garvey cut him off. "It's not all mine. I gotta pay back Owen. That was the plan from the beginning. I was gonna run my car off the bridge, hide out for a few months till Tess could have me declared dead. She was going to collect the insurance money. Then she was supposed to meet me in Belle Glade. I was staying there in a little hotel near the airport since the accident. She was supposed to rent a car, pick me up, and then the two of us were supposed to drive to Orlando. I knew a guy there that had gotten me a fake driver's license and passport. Then we were going to drive down to the Keys, and then charter a boat to Nassau. Then a flight from there to the Dominican. Once we settled in somewhere, I was going to have Tess wire Owen the money I took.

Then one day I pick up the Belle Glade *Sun*, and there's my obituary, along with a little story about the accident and me being declared dead. I wasn't supposed to contact Tess, she was supposed to contact me. But she never did. I waited till the following Monday, still never heard anything from her. I guess curiosity got the best of me. I took a bus back to Miami, and went to my own funeral in disguise. I had on a fake mustache, dark glasses, a hat, the works. There was Tess, Owen, his wife, and a few other friends and family, all crying at my graveside. It's really something, witnessing your own funeral, Dan."

"I bet it is Garvey," Dan replied.

"So anyway," Garvey continued, "I got a cab and followed her back to the house. Guess who met her at the door with a big kiss and a hug?"

"Jeff Hinder," Dan answered.

"You got it. That bastard was living in my house, with my wife. A couple hours later they came out of the house with suitcases packed, got in her car and drove away."

"How did you know they came here?" Dan asked.

Garvey downed the remainder of his drink. "After they left the house, I went in. First thing I did was go to the computer and look through the history. There were searches for hotels in Key West and a route they had mapped out to get here. She never did clear her history, that's how I found out about her affair the first time. Then I checked a couple places in the house where I had a couple grand stashed in case of an emergency and called my buddy in Orlando. He met me halfway with my new identity. I rented a car and headed down here. The only problem was, the credit card I used to rent the car was stolen, so I could only use it once." Garvey lowered his head shamefully and added, "I'm running out of cash, Coast, and I haven't got anywhere to stay."

"You can stay here till we figure out what to do," Dan told Garvey.

"That would be great, thanks."

"So what then? What did you do after you got here?" Dan asked.

"Well, I knew where they were staying, because they booked it online. I checked myself into a little hotel down the street from theirs. I went over to their hotel and snooped around Monday night; there was no sign of them. Tuesday, they went to a place not far from here and rented jet skis for a few hours. I followed them all over the island. As I followed them I became more and more pissed off."

"Pissed off enough to kill someone?" Dan asked.

"No, just pissed off. They were acting as if they were doing nothing wrong, like a couple on their honeymoon or something. Tess sure wasn't acting like a woman that had just buried her husband. It was driving me crazy. I kept thinking, how am I going to get that money back? So I decided to stir things up a little."

"That's when you made the call to Hinder at their hotel," Dan suggested.

"Yes. I figured I only had a couple days since it looked like their plan was the same as mine. So I made the call."

Dan got up to make another drink; Garvey stuck out his glass for a refill.

"What did you say to Hinder?" Dan asked from the bar. "According to the desk clerk, he looked pretty frightened."

"I told him I was on the island, I knew where he was staying, and I was on my way to kill him. I knew I could say whatever I wanted, there was no way he was going to the police. I hoped he would get spooked and leave the hotel and leave Tess there alone so I could talk to her. And that's just what he did."

Dan returned with the drinks. "So then you went to the hotel to talk to Tess?"

"No. First I followed Hinder to see where he would go."

"And where did he go?" Dan asked.

"That's where things started to get really strange. He took a cab to a hotel on the other side of the island, the Laguna Inn. When he got there, he didn't check in. He went right to one of the rooms and knocked on the door. A young woman, brunette, probably mid-twenties, opened the door and let him in."

Dan folded his arms in front of him and touched his glass to his chin. "Well, we know where he's staying, and we know he isn't leaving the island without that money. We just gotta find it first. So when did you finally speak to Tess?"

"I never spoke to her till Friday. A little while after you created that little scene at the bar."

"Oh yeah. It worked didn't it?" Dan chuckled.

"It worked alright. I went right from the bar to Tess's hotel. When I got there she was sitting at the bar. As you can imagine she was pretty startled to see me. I walked over and sat down beside her. She was in shock."

"Tell me about the meeting, Garvey," Dan said. "And don't leave anything out."

"Don't worry," said Garvey. "I remember it word for word."

*****

"How did you find me?" Tess asked.

"How did I find you?" Garvey replied, "I'm the one that came up with this plan, did you forget that? Only it was supposed to be me and you, not you and him. How could you do this to me? I loved you."

"You didn't love me. You loved your work, and then you loved gambling. Where did I fit in? We lost everything because of you. I have nothing now."

"Nothing Tess?" Garvey responded. "I think you have something. Eight hundred thousand dollars. Where's my money, Tess?"

"It's my money, Tim. That policy was in my name; the check was in my name."

"But I'm not dead, Tess. If I go to the cops, you'll end up having to give the money back anyway. Were you even going to give Owen his money back?"

"Why should I, I didn't steal from him, you did."

"And now I'm going to pay him back, and I need that money to do it. So where is the money Tess?" Garvey asked once again.

"I hid it. I hid it where only I can find it. It's all mine."

"All yours? What about Jeff Hinder? It looked like you were planning to share some of it with him."

"Jeff loves me, Tim. He treats me like you never did. He makes me feel like you never could."

"If he loves you so much, then why is he shacked up on the other side of the island with some other woman?"

"You're lying!"

"No, I'm not lying, and if I were you, I would quiet down. We don't want to cause a scene and have the cops called. They would probably start asking questions. Questions you wouldn't want to answer. Now why don't you tell why the love of your life would be checked into a hotel with another woman, or is this a part of the plan that you didn't know about?"

"Where is he, Tim? Where is Jeff?" Tess asked, with tears in her eyes.

"I'll bring you there, and then you bring me to the money," Garvey said.

*****

"…And that's what I did." Garvey said, finishing up his story. "We went up to her room, she changed, and I drove her over to the Laguna Inn. We parked across the street, so we could watch Jeff's hotel room door. We sat there in the car for about an hour, just talking. It had been a long time since we had just talked. As Tess talked, she watched the door to Hinder's motel room, and I watched her face, her eyes. I was looking for something. I don't know what. Maybe a sign of the Tess I once knew. Then I saw the color leave her face. I turned toward the motel and there was Hinder leaving the room with the other woman. My first thought was, how does it feel, Tess? How does it feel to be betrayed by someone you love and trust? Then a feeling of sympathy. I knew what it felt like to be betrayed by the person you love, and now that she felt it too, I felt bad for her."

"Touching," Dan added. "What then?"

"She told me to drive away. She said she couldn't face him. I drove her back to my hotel. We ordered room service. While we ate, we talked some more. She agreed to pay back Owen, and then split the remainder of the money with me. I figured that was better than nothing. We planned to spend the night at my place, and then I would drive her to pick up the money in the morning.

After dinner, she said she wanted to be alone, go for a little walk. That's the last time I saw her. That was Friday evening. The next morning when I awoke, I could see the cop cars and ambulance." Garvey's eyes misted over. "I walked over and spoke to some people who told me a woman had been found dead on the beach."

"Smather's Beach is only a few hundred yards from your hotel. So she probably walked there. The question is, how did she end up dead?" Dan asked.

Dan got up from the dining room chair and headed back to the kitchen for aspirin. His tequila bottle induced headache was returning, and his back was stiffening up from his extended stay in the hard-wooden chair.

Like Pavlov's dog hearing a bell, Buddy also headed for the kitchen. If Dan was eating, so was Buddy. When Dan noticed Buddy hot on his trail, he walked to the refrigerator and grabbed a few slices of lunchmeat and tossed them in Buddy's vicinity. Buddy snatched them out of the air and, quickly swallowing them whole, turned and headed back toward his bed.

"Ya know what I don't get, Garvey?" Dan yelled from the kitchen. "How did Hinder find Tess at the beach?"

There was no answer from the living room. Dan walked back in.

"Garvey?" he said.

Garvey was gone, his empty glass sitting on the end table beside the chair he had occupied.

"Son of a bitch!" Dan cursed, as he looked toward Buddy, trying to get comfortable in his bed, "You couldn't have told me he was leaving?"

The dog whimpered, tried a few more positions, and finally settled down on the bed.

"For crying out loud, dog, you look about as comfortable as a whore in church," Dan said. "If that bed ain't comfortable enough for you, you're shit out of luck."

Dan walked to his front door and opened the screen. He walked out onto the front porch and into his front yard. Looking up the street one way and then the other, he simply said to himself, "Huh, didn't see that coming."

When he walked back into the house Buddy was already asleep. He grabbed his drink off the dining room table and headed to his chair. The TV insert lay open on the armrest. Dan picked it up, scanned the listings, and smiled. He flipped the power on from the remote, punched in Me-TV, and pulled up the footrest on the La-Z-Boy as the synthesized theme from *The Rockford Files* lifted his spirits.

"Ah, Jim Rockford. I wonder how many times he got hit in the head with a bottle of tequila." Dan yawned.

He looked over at Buddy snoring away. "That many times, huh?"

Chapter Twenty-Seven

Coast awoke in the chair he had fallen asleep in. His rocks glass sat on the table next to Garvey's. The ice in both had long since melted. The TV was still on. The sweaty, muscle-bound pitchman on the screen was telling Dan how he could lose thirty pounds in thirty days, and have six pack abs. All he had to do was lay back on this stupid looking piece of plastic shit, and rock back and forth. *Now I know why Elvis liked to shoot out the screen when the mood took him.* He picked up the remote and began to surf through the channels.

As he jumped from channel to channel, he thought back to the days when he would turn to the Weather Channel first thing every morning. Now, living in this tropical paradise as he did, there was no reason to watch a channel about weather, unless perhaps it was hurricane season. But that was months away, and today would be sunny and warm just like almost every other day.

Buddy walked slowly into the kitchen with Dan leading the way. Dan turned toward the coffee pot as Buddy turned toward the chrome colored dish that bore his name and sat waiting patiently. Dan poured a cup of coffee, smelled it, and dumped it in the sink. He slid out the tray to reveal the mold covered coffee grounds.

"Look at this, Buddy, we got our own science experiment going on here," Dan observed.

Dan searched through the cupboard for a can of coffee; when he found it, he went through the steps, and pushed the start button. He then turned his attention to Buddy, fed and watered him, then poured his cup of coffee. He sipped the coffee and made the usual *holy shit that's strong* face and headed for the front porch, where he knew his morning paper would be waiting.

Sitting in the lawn chair by the fire pit, Dan drank his coffee and flipped through the Citizen, as Buddy played on the beach.

Dan heard Buddy barking and looked up from his paper. It was the young couple from last week. They were throwing a stick for Buddy to fetch, and Buddy was playing the model canine, something he usually only did around others. Dan watched as the three played on the beach. The young woman looked up, and noticing Dan, walked over toward him with Buddy close behind.

"Is this your dog?" she asked

"No," Dan replied, "it's my wife's."

The girl patted Buddy's head. "Beautiful dog."

"You want him?"

"Sure!" the young girl laughed.

Christ, I'd hate to listen to that laugh all day, Dan observed. *And stop flicking your hair like that. Everyone can see you have long blonde hair just as clear as we can see you have almost no breasts whatsoever.*

By this time the young man had also walked over to join in the morning conversation.

"Great dog, sir," the boy said.

"So I've heard," Dan returned.

"He sure is friendly. I bet he doesn't make a very good guard dog," the young man said.

"You have no idea," Dan said straight-faced.

"You live here?" the girl asked.

"Yup."

"Wow, it was great being here for a week," the boy enthused, all teeth and bony shoulders. "It must be awesome living here."

To Dan, the boy looked like he had just stepped out of a Kohl's circular in the Sunday paper. Young idiot's department.

"Oh, it's awesome," Dan replied.

"We're on our honeymoon," The girl announced. "We have to leave tomorrow."

Why not now? "That's too bad," Dan said.

It was about this time that Dan started working on a plan that would get him out of this seemingly never-ending chit chat. Suddenly he looked where his watch would be if he wore one.

"Oh, wow, look at the time," Coast blurted out. "I better get going. It was nice meeting you both. You kids have a safe trip back to…to."

"New York," the boy interjected.

"Swell," Dan said under his breath, as he turned and quickly headed back up the gravel pathway to his back door.

When he got to the screen door he held it open for Buddy, and looked down, but Buddy wasn't there. Dan turned back toward the yard to see that Buddy had returned to his game of fetch with his new friends.

"Traitor," Dan said as he went through the door.

Coast knew where Hinder was hiding out and had decided the night before that it might be time to pay him a little visit. So, after showering, getting dressed and luring Buddy away from his new family, he decided to take a trip out to the Laguna Inn.

As he walked toward the door, he suddenly stopped, turned around, and headed toward his bedroom, and then to his closet. Dan knelt down, pulled the carpet back, and pulled up a loose floorboard, to reveal a small case hidden in a compartment underneath. Dan removed the case from its hiding place and opened it. Inside was a pistol. A .45 caliber M1911 single action, semi-automatic.

Dan had purchased the weapon three years earlier for seven hundred dollars from a young gentleman in an alley in Miami. Dan had never fired the gun, and it had only been out of the case on two drunken occasions when he had decided that he had lived in the past long enough. On both occasions the gun had been put back a few hours later when it had become evident to him that he was just too much of a coward to end his own life.

In the case next to the gun was a box of .45 caliber shells. Dan removed the magazine from the grip, removed the bullets from their box, and loaded the weapon. When he was finished, he stood up and placed the weapon between his waistband and the small of his back. Dan had never had a weapon in this position before, but had seen the move in every cop film he had ever watched.

Dan walked over to the liquor shelf and. chose a bottle. He poured a shot of Johnny Walker Red, took a deep breath, and downed it. He poured another and downed it. He set the shot glass back on the bar and turned toward the front door. As he walked past buddy, he crouched and patted him on the head.

"See ya in a little while, pal."

Buddy licked Dan's hand and put his head down on his bed.

Dan walked out onto his front porch, just as Don, *the asshole*, was pulling up in front. Don had a bottle wrapped in a brown paper bag. He took a drink and opened the car door. He was talking to himself and tripped as he made his way toward the house.

"Have you seen that whore anywheres?" he called out to Dan. "Her car's not here. She must be out screwing somebody."

He staggered into the house, as Dan followed with his eyes. Dan shook his head and moved slowly toward his own car. He opened the door and stopped. He looked back toward Bev's house. Dan gently closed the door, not making a sound, and began walking toward Bev's. When he got to the door, he quietly opened it and went in.

He stood in the center of the living room and listened as Don made another unneeded drink. First, he heard the ice hit the glass, then the booze being poured in. All the while Don talked to himself about the whore who was lucky to have him.

Dan looked around the room. There were no pictures of Frank anywhere. He wondered if Don made her take them down. This angered Dan even more. Dan heard the drunk's footsteps as he approached the living room.

"What the hell are you doing in my house?" Don yelled.

"Your house?" Dan countered.

"Yeah, my house. Getta hell outta my houshe." Don's words were slurred. Dan walked toward Don, pulling the gun from its resting place. Don's eyes widened, and he instantly sobered up.

"Wh, what are you going to do with that?" Don asked, his voice shaking.

Dan lifted the hand with the gun and planted it on the side of Don's head with a swift blow. The drunk fell backward to the floor. Dan kept walking toward him. Don was crawling backwards, trying to escape what he thought might be the end. When his shoulders hit the wall behind him, he knew he was trapped. He stared up at the angry man above him, waiting to see what was next. Dan knelt in front of him.

"Open your mouth," Dan said quietly.

"Whaaaat?"

"Open your fucking mouth!" Dan yelled.

The trapped animal opened its mouth. Dan slid the top of the barrel back, cocking the hammer, and placed the gun into Don's mouth. Don sat very still, but shaking slightly as a bead of sweat dripped down his forehead. Dan spoke very slowly and calmly, so Don would understand every word.

"She's not a whore, you piece of shit. She's a wonderful, beautiful person, and so was her husband. You're not. If I ever hear any yelling coming from this house ever again, I'm coming back over here, putting this gun back in your mouth, and blowing off your god damn head. Do you understand me?"

Don slowly moved his head up and down.

"Do you think I'm joking?" Dan asked.

Don slowly moved his head from side to side.

"Good. I'm glad we've come to some kind of an agreement. Also, if I were you, I would keep this entire conversation to myself. Oh yeah, and Don, if you don't think you're going to be able to follow these simple guidelines, then you might want to start looking for another place to live."

Dan stood up and walked out. As he walked toward his car, he placed the .45 back in his waistband. He was grinning from ear to ear. He had hated Don for a long time, and that conversation felt really good, so good the grin didn't leave his face until he was in his car and halfway to the Laguna Inn.

Chapter Twenty-Eight

Coast pulled up across the street from the Laguna Inn. It was a quiet Wednesday, warm, a little before noon. He parked behind a row of green garbage cans. They were empty. Down the street he saw a propane dealership. There were three motorcycles parked halfway down the block. Across the street from the motorcycles, a cop was writing a parking ticket and placing it under the windshield wiper of a blue F-250 attached to an empty boat trailer. Two children kicked a ball back and forth at the edge of the road.

The Laguna was not the kind of motel that would be bustling with tourists. It was more a place where a crack addict or a meth head would go to do their drug of choice, or maybe a boss would go to do their secretary of choice. It was a one-story hotel, with an office at the far end of the building. The roof, in the front, had a four-foot overhang that was held up by wrought iron posts. Underneath the overhang was a sidewalk that ran the full length of the building. Each room had a front door that exited out into the parking lot, and a back door that went out to the pool. The pool, which hadn't seen fresh water in at least five years, was starting to resemble an overgrown Petri dish. It was a breeding ground for mosquitoes and a trap for the occasional turtle. Dan was surprised the city hadn't cited the Laguna's owners. The building was made of cement blocks and painted white, but hadn't been painted in years. There was no grass anywhere on the property.

Dan didn't know what room Hinder was in, or who the mystery girl was Jeff Hinder was staying with. Garvey hadn't stuck around long enough to answer those questions. However, he did know what Hinder looked like, and Hinder was going to wish he had hit Dan hard enough to cause amnesia.

Dan sat out front watching the hotel for about an hour when a woman exited Room 25. A brunette, a tall brunette, a familiar tall brunette. It was Karen. At that moment Dan knew his encounter with her wasn't by chance. It was a setup. She was at the Atlantic Inn for a reason. She was at his house for a reason too. Now it was becoming all too obvious. She was there to find the suitcase, the money. No wonder a good-looking woman like that was so eager to go home with a dishwasher. It wasn't the dishwasher as much as it was the home she wanted to see.

The more he thought about it, the more pissed he became with himself. *Why hadn't I caught on? How did she fool me?* A beautiful face can really cloud your judgment. Dan knew he would be getting back at her soon enough. The death of a boyfriend can be pretty traumatic.

Dan slumped down in the seat, out of sight. She walked toward a car, a red Ford Escort, unlocked it with a remote, and grabbed something off the dashboard. Dan reached for the glove compartment, opened it and took out a small pair of binoculars. Now he could see she retrieved a pack of cigarettes. His eyes went from Karen to the car. On the bumper was a small sticker: "Drive-Rite Auto Rentals". Then she went to the soda vending machine at the end of the building, then back to her room, where she was met at the door by none other than Jeff Hinder, douche bag extraordinaire.

Maybe this wasn't the right time to bust into Hinder's room, guns a blastin', Dan mused. After all, this ain't Tombstone, and I definitely ain't Wyatt Earp. Maybe when he is alone.

But how was he going to get him alone. *No need to rush this thing, Hinder's not going anywhere, that's for sure. He's not leaving without Garvey's money.*

Dan started his Porsche and headed toward Red's for a drink and something to eat.

Chapter Twenty-Nine

It was a little before two by the time he got to Red's. Dan hadn't eaten breakfast, or lunch, and he was starving.

Wednesday night was all-you-could-eat crab legs and sirloin steak. Dinner didn't start until four, but Dan could smell steak cooking already, which meant Red couldn't wait till dinner to have one of Jock's fantastic steaks. Dan's mouth was watering as he crossed the parking lot. He was hoping there was one on the grill for him as well.

"God, that smells good," Dan said as he walked through the kitchen doors, "I hope there's one with my name on it."

"Well, no, but there was two for me," Red replied from behind the grill. "So I guess now there is one for me and one for you."

Red put each steak on a plate, French fries, and made his way back to the dining room to a table in the corner. The table he would always refer to as "his table." Dan headed to the cooler and grabbed them each a beer, and joined Red.

"What, no crab legs?" Dan asked.

Red frowned. "Just eat your steak, for Christ sakes."

"Just kidding, Red."

Red dumped half a bottle of A1 on his steak and took a big bite. "So, Columbo, how's the case going?"

"It's not a case, Red, and it's not going that well. I did figure out why neither man wants to leave the island. There's money, and a lot of it. There's no mystery though. As far as Hinder, there's no proof, but he probably killed Tess, and as far as the missing boyfriend, he's not missing anymore. The dead husband, that mystery is solved. The only thing we don't know is, where the money is, and the only person that knows the answer to that is dead."

"So there's almost a million dollars hid here somewhere on the island, and two different men want it," Red offered.

"Four different men want it," Dan corrected his friend.

"Are you keeping it if you find it, Dan?"

"Not all of it, but I was hired to find a woman's boyfriend, and I found him. I'm gonna get paid for it, and I'm gonna get a little extra for my pain and suffering," Dan answered.

"Oh yeah, the bottle upside the head. So, who's the fourth guy that wants it?" Red asked.

"Garvey's partner, Owen Reeves."

"Oh yeah, I forgot about him. So what are ya gonna do now? Are ya going to Rick and let him know what's going on?"

"I can't go to Rick yet. He'll just arrest Garvey for fraud, and question Hinder about Tess's death. There's no proof anyone murdered her, so Rick won't hold him. Then the island will be full of people looking everywhere for the money. As soon as someone finds it, it'll be given back to the insurance company for a small reward. Then Garvey's partner is out the two hundred thousand, I'm out my reward, and you're out nineteen bucks for this steak. We have to do this quiet, so everyone gets what's coming to them."

Red glanced around the empty restaurant. "We?"

"Yeah, we. I can't do this on my own. We have to retrace her steps, figure out where she put that money. Maybe she left a note or told someone where she put it. I'm heading home. I'll swing by your house around nine tomorrow morning. You can go with me to talk to Garvey at his hotel, if he's still there. Then I want to stop by the Atlantic Inn and find out what they did with Tess's belongings."

Red loved an adventure. "Sounds good, Dan. I'll see you in the morning."

Chapter Thirty

Dan pulled into his driveway, turned off the car, and reached into the glove box. He pulled out the pistol he had placed there before going into Red's. He looked around to make sure no one was watching and walked into his house.

Buddy was not home again, and Dan wondered where he had been spending his evenings. Even though Buddy and Dan didn't have the kind of relationship most men and their dogs have, Dan still found a certain comfort knowing Buddy would be home to greet him when he came in. Buddy was also just the kind of TV watching partner that Dan loved. Buddy never complained about what they watched, never spoke during the important parts, and never asked any questions about the plot line. Now, however, Buddy was spending time elsewhere, and Dan felt abandoned.

He walked to the fridge, grabbed a couple beers, and headed to his chairs by the fire pit. On his way out, he noticed Bev sitting on her back steps. It looked as though she had been crying.

"Bev!" Dan called out to her, holding up one of the beers in the air as an offering.

"No thanks, Dan, I just want to be alone," Bev hollered.

"Well, maybe *I* don't want to be alone Bev. So just maybe you would be doing me a big favor if you came over here and drank one of these beers with me."

"Well, if you're going to twist my arm, neighbor."

Bev got up from her steps and walked over toward the chairs in Dan's backyard. A trip she had made so many times in the past, but not so often lately. She was walking over alone, something she was not used to doing. Most of these trips from her yard to Dan's had been with Frank. As she got closer Dan could see the loneliness in her eyes. He could feel the pain she was feeling. The loss that the two of them shared was a horrible bond that no two people should ever share, but at the same time they could provide comfort for one another. Dan was glad she came over and it showed in his smile. She smiled too.

"Long time no see, neighbor," Bev said as she settled into the lawn chair.

"My thoughts exactly. So where's Don tonight?" Dan asked as he twisted the top off of one of the beers and handed it to Bev.

Her voice was hollow. "He left me, Dan."

"Left you? Did he say why?" Dan asked, knowing full well he may have had something to do with the departure.

"He said things weren't going the way he wanted them to. He wasn't happy. He gave me the old 'it's not you it's me' story."

"What did you say?"

"I told him he was right, it wasn't me, it was him!"

They both laughed out loud at Bev's remark, but Bev's laughter quickly turned to tears as she put her face in the palm of her hands and shook her head back and forth.

"What's wrong with me, Dan? Why would I have ever let a man like that into my life, into my home, into Frank's home?"

"I don't know, Bev. Maybe you were just looking for someone to fill that void in your life left by Frank," Dan reassured her. "I think we both know Don never could have replaced Frank."

"I know. I don't know what I was thinking. I was just so lonely."

"I know Bev. I miss him too."

Dan built up a fire in the pit, and they sat for hours, telling stories and laughing about the days when the three of them would sit by the fire until the sun came up. They told stories that Frank used to tell; they told some of his jokes, and even sang some of his dirty schoolboy songs. They both had heard them so many times they could recite them word for word with no problem at all. When one told a joke the other would laugh. When one would start a song, the other would join in. Each story would start with the same line: Remember the time? When no one was talking they would just sit and stare into the fire and remember.

As the fire burned down lower and lower, Dan poked a stick at the embers. As the fire faded away so did the evening. Dan stretched, and Bev yawned.

"Wow, it's getting pretty late. Old people like me shouldn't be out this late," said Bev, adopting a creaky old woman voice. "I better be getting in."

"Are you going to be alright over there alone?" Dan asked.

"Don't you worry about me, pal. I'm a big girl. I'll see you tomorrow," Bev replied with a slight grin.

With that, Bev headed back to her house. Dan poured the last of his beer on the coals. He called out to Buddy and whistled a few times, but there was no response, so he went into his house just as alone as his friend and neighbor went to hers.

When he got to his living room, he looked at the blank TV screen, and then looked to the remote. After careful consideration, he decided to sleep in his bed tonight. Something he rarely did alone.

Chapter Thirty-One

"Mr. Coast?" came a deep, authoritative voice from the phone.

"Yes," Dan replied

"Dan Coast?"

"Yes. Who is this?"

"Mr. Coast, this is Trooper Stevens, with the New York State Police. Mr. Coast there's been an accident."

Dan felt the hairs on the back of his neck bristle. "An accident? What are you talking about?"

"It's your wife Mr. Coast. She was in an automobile accident this afternoon. Can you come down to the hospital, Mr. Coast?" the voice on the other end said.

"Is she okay?" Dan asked, already knowing from the urgency in the officer's shaky voice that she was not okay.

"I think it's better if you just come down to the hospital and speak with the doctors, Mr. Coast."

Dan arrived at the hospital in less than fifteen minutes, a drive that would have usually taken around twenty-five minutes by someone obeying the traffic signals, and someone not driving a brand new Porsche. This was no time to follow rules. This was surely no time for any man to even be behind the wheel. He pulled his car up close to the emergency room entrance and parked in a space that read, "Ambulance parking only, all others will be towed at owner's expense," having his car towed was the last thing on Dan's mind.

As he raced through the automatic doors, a man in a white uniform yelled, "Hey pal, you can't park there." Dan ignored the man and ran up to the first person sitting at a desk he saw.

"My wife was brought in. She was in a car accident. Where do I go?"

"Can I have your name, sir?" the nurse asked.

"Dan Coast, my wife's name is Alex, Alex Coast."

"Let me call a doctor for you Mr. Coast," she said as she read her computer screen.

Dan pounded the desk with his fist and yelled, "Just tell me where she is, dammit!"

Just then a doctor and a police officer emerged through a set of swinging doors.

"Mr. Coast?" said the doctor in a quiet, somber tone. A tone of voice that didn't put Dan at ease, but only added to his fears.

"Yes, I'm Dan Coast. Where's my wife?"

"I'm sorry, Mr. Coast. Your wife didn't make it. We did everything we could. I'm... I'm very sorry."

"How... what happened?" Dan asked as he looked toward the officer.

"We're not sure, Mr. Coast. Your wife's car was the only vehicle involved. It looks like she just swerved and hit the guard rails. There was a dog in the car, the way he was positioned after the wreck, we think he may have jumped on her lap, and got caught in the steering wheel."

An EMT walked through the emergency room doors with Buddy on a leash. The man walked toward Dan. As they drew closer, Buddy shied away from Dan. The dog had a look on his face Dan knew all too well. It was the same look he had when he got in the garbage or chewed up a shoe. It was as if Buddy knew what he had done.

"Here's your dog, sir. I just took him for a walk around the hospital to calm him down," the EMT said.

Dan stared at Buddy. "There's not a mark on him,"

The EMT patted the dog's head. "No, he's going to be just fine."

"You say that like it's a good thing." Dan replied as he took the leash from the man.

"If you're ready to see your wife, Mr. Coast, please come with me," said the doctor gently.

A nurse entering the room said, "Sir, you can't have a dog in here." The police officer shot her an angry look and raised his hand to silence her.

Dan, along with Buddy, followed the doctor to a large exam room partitioned off by several curtains. The doctor slid back the first curtain. There on the bed was the still shape of Dan's wife, with the sheet pulled up over her face. Dan approached. With his right hand he held Buddy's leash, and with his left he slowly pulled back the sheet to reveal his wife's face.

Even up to this point Dan was still hoping that this was all a horrible mistake and that he would pull back the sheet and see someone else. Perhaps he would see someone that his wife had loaned her car to. But no, it was his wife. She looked as though she was sleeping. The only flaw on her perfect face was a small cut above her eye that had been cleaned by a nurse in anticipation of a husband's arrival.

Dan handed the leash to the police officer.

"Can you take him, just for a second? I want to be alone with her for a minute." Dan requested.

"Sure, Mr. Coast, take your time," the officer responded.

Dan leaned over and kissed Alex on the forehead, and then buried his face in her neck, all the while stroking her hair. He stayed in the same position for a long while, knowing that this would be the last time he would hold his wife. She still smelled like his wife. He could smell her perfume, Eternity. Dan remembered the first time he ever saw her. She was standing at a stove making scrambled eggs. She was in college and renting a room in a building where Dan was working. She was the most beautiful woman he had ever seen in his life. He remembered the instant their eyes met. He remembered her smile. He knew he would never smell her perfume again.

When he finally lifted his head, he stood and stared at her face. *You're the most beautiful woman in the world.* He noticed the wet stain his tears had left on her shoulder.

"I love you, Princess," he whispered, as he stroked her arm, turned, and walked away.

Dan walked back into the waiting room and sat down in a chair. Buddy walked over to him and tried to lick his face.

Dan pushed him away roughly. "Go on, dog, get away from me."

Buddy didn't listen; he kept trying to lick Dan's face.

"Go on, dog, get away from me. Go on, dog."

*****

Dan awoke with a start, and repeated one more time to himself, "Go on, dog."

Dan lay in his bed, wet from sweat. He rubbed his eyes and looked around the room. Buddy was sitting next to him with his head cocked to one side, trying to figure out what he had done wrong, and why he was telling him to go away.

Dan looked at the alarm clock on the nightstand.

"Crap! It's nine-fifteen. Why didn't you wake me up, dog?"

Dan rolled over, opened the nightstand drawer and took out the .45 he had placed there before going to bed. He pointed the gun at Buddy, sighting the gun between the dog's eyes. He made a child's sound of a bullet being fired. Buddy just sat and stared at Dan, looking like the RCA Victor dog. Dan lowered the gun and laid it on the bed.

"God damn dog," he sighed.

Chapter Thirty-Two

Dan Coast took a right off Thompson Street onto Rose Street, took a quick right, and pulled into Red's driveway, to the distant strains of "Aloha Oe." Red was sitting on his front steps, with a not so happy look on his face. As Dan pulled in, Red walked to the passenger side of Dan's car.

"Been waiting long?" Dan asked.

"Only since the time that you told me you would be here," Red groused. "That's okay, though, I love sitting here listening to that idiot next door play his ukulele. Does he know this isn't Hawaii, Dan? Someday I'm gonna go over there and shove that thing where he can't possibly reach the strings."

"I'm guessing you haven't had your coffee this morning, Red."

Grunting, Red tried to open the passenger side door, but it wouldn't budge.

"Oh yeah, you gotta climb over," Dan advised him. "That door quit working the other day."

Red climbed over the door just the way you would imagine a large man would. He sat down and buckled his seat belt without a sound, except for the sound of Dan laughing through pursed lips.

As they drove along Dan filled Red in on the plans of the day. Where they would go, who they would talk to, and what they might be looking for.

Dan felt far more comfortable with Red along for the ride. Red might seem like a pushover, like a teddy bear on the outside, but Dan had seen him throw more than a few drunken troublemakers out of his bar. Red was a basically gentle and soft-spoken man. He could tolerate a lot of people's ignorance right up to the point where his cool was lost. At that point it was usually a good idea to take cover or wind up being what Phil Lambert referred to one night as *collateral damage*.

"Coffee, Red?" Dan asked his partner of the day.

"That sounds good."

Dan pulled the car off to the side of the road and found a parking spot in front of Joe's Joe. Unlike Red's, the owner really was named Joe. Dan and Red went in.

"What's up Molly?" Red said, winking at the young girl behind the counter. She wore a baby blue retro 50s-style bib apron trimmed with red hearts. Her naturally pretty face, Betty Page haircut, and saucy personality made her the most popular waitress at Joe's.

"Not much," Molly said. "Good morning, Dan, how are you today?"

"Wonderful!" Dan replied.

"I'm fine too," Red chimed in.

"What can I get you?" Molly asked Dan.

"The usual, Molly. To go."

"You got it, ace," Molly replied, grabbing a large togo cup from a stack next to the register.

"I'll have the usual too, Molly," Red said.

Molly spun to face him. "What's that again, sir?"

"Large coffee, with cream and sugar, Molly. I'm in here three times a week since this place opened for Chrissake. This guy's in here maybe once a month," Red jerked his thumb rudely at Dan, who was busting a gut laughing, "and you remember *his* usual."

"Sorry, Red," Molly apologized, as she handed Dan his coffee with a wink. "Here ya go, Dan. Now what was that again, Red? Large decaf with what?"

Red enunciated each word slowly through his teeth. "Large. Regular. With. Cream. And. Sugar!"

Molly filled his cup and said, "Here ya go, Red. I promise I'll remember the next time."

"That's what you said the last time, and where's *my* wink?" Red mumbled, as they headed for the car.

The awkward exchange between Red and Molly provided plenty of material for the conversation from Joe's to the Atlantic Inn. Red always seemed to have some story about a female conquest, or some girl who was in love with him. Yet rarely did anyone seem to be around to witness these encounters, and there was nothing funnier to Dan than watching Red try and prove his self-proclaimed title of ladies' man. Dan knew exactly how far he could dish the ribbing before Red went postal, and he never missed a chance to push right up to that point.

"Molly's a nice-looking girl," said Dan. "I bet a stud like you would have no trouble hitting that. 'Course, she wouldn't remember your name in the morning, or what you liked in your coffee for that matter."

"Very funny, very funny," Red said as they pulled up to the valet at the Atlantic Inn.

"Don't scratch it, Billy," Dan said as he tossed the keys to the valet.

"Sure thing, Mr. Coast."

"It's Dan, Billy."

"Sure thing, Mr. Coast."

"How's it going Billy?" Red asked.

Billy eyed him with a puzzled look. "Good …er, uh…sir."

"Mr. Baxter," Red fumed.

"Oh yeah. Good, Mr. Baxter."

"Don't start," Red said as he looked at a smiling Dan.

Dan and Red walked up to the front desk, Dan still grinning, Red, not so much. Dan recognized the young man behind the desk as being the same young man he had spoken to before. When the young man saw Dan walking toward him, he smiled and put the palms of his hands together under his chin.

"Well, if it isn't Daniel Coast," The young man lisped. "And to what do I owe this unexpected surprise? Are you here on business again, or did you just miss me?"

"I did miss you, but I am here on business, Michael," Dan replied, glancing at the young man's name tag.

Michael beamed. "You remembered my name, Daniel!"

"How could I forget?" Dan said with a grin.

"So, what can I do for you today, Daniel?" the clerk asked. "Are you staking out a perp, or maybe tailing a serial killer?"

"No, nothing that exciting. We're just here to see what happened to Mrs. Garvey's personal effects. Maybe take a look through them."

Michael leaned forward and spoke in a confidential whisper. "I would let you, Daniel, if they were here. But the police picked up her stuff, the day after you were here. Then the next day, the man she left with came and tried to pick up her stuff. Turns out he was her husband." He paused and added in a soft purr, "I was going to call you and let you know all this, but you never gave me your phone number."

Red looked sick to his stomach. "Look, Dan, why don't we just go ask Rick if we can look through her stuff?"

"Because I don't want him to know I'm still involved in this," Dan replied. "We better just head over to Garvey's hotel and ask him what it was he was looking for in her belongings."

"Thanks for your help, Michael," Dan said as he and Red turned to walk away.

"You're welcome, Daniel. If you need anything, you know where I am," Michael said, fluttering his hand.

"Is there anything you want to tell me about you and Michael, Daniel?" Red teased as they headed toward the door.

Chapter Thirty-Three

Dan and Red pulled up in front of the Ocean Breeze Hotel. Nicer than the Laguna Inn, but nowhere near as nice as the Atlantic Inn. The Ocean Breeze was a few blocks from the water. It was a nice place that catered mostly to families on a budget. Similar to the Laguna it was one long building, but two stories. The office was on the first floor, halfway down the building. The pool at the Ocean Breeze had real water.

"Garvey must have brought a little more money with him on his trip than Hinder did. He's got a lot nicer hotel," Red said jokingly.

Dan nodded. "He must have. But he told me he was almost out of money. He probably thought he would get his hands on the insurance money a little faster than he has."

The two men parked and went into the office. When they got to the counter Dan began pulling little slips of paper from his pocket, some with addresses, some with names, and finally what he was searching for, the picture of Garvey. Dan showed it to the desk clerk.

"Is this man staying here?" Dan asked.

"Who's asking?" the clerk responded.

"I am," Dan barked. "I'm Detective Phil Fish with the police department, and this man is wanted for questioning in a murder investigation."

The clerk's eyes widened. "Sorry, yeah, he's staying here. He's in room …um, let's see," he riffled through the logbook. "Room 116."

"Do you know if he's here?" Red asked.

Dan caught the clerk's confused look and offered, "This is my forensics guy, Dr. Quincy."

The clerk nodded and said, "No, his cars not here, he must have left. My shift started about an hour ago. He's been gone at least that long."

"Is he current with his bill?" Dan asked.

"Yes, he paid for two more nights yesterday afternoon."

"Very good. Now, are you going to cooperate, and let us in his room to have a look around, or should I make a couple calls and have this place shut down while I get a search warrant?" Dan asked.

The clerk looked frantic. "No, that won't be necessary, I'll let you in. Let me get the key."

Dan and Red followed the clerk to Garvey's room. Red turned to Dan and whispered.

"'I'm with the police department?' You could get into some deep shit for saying that. Lucky this guy is too dumb to ask for IDs."

"What? I am with the police department," replied Dan, grinning. "As a law abiding citizen, I think we all are. If you're not with them you're against them, right?" Dan responded with a grin.

"Ya got me there," Red said, shaking his head.

"Here ya go," the clerk said, opening the door. "Lock up when ya leave."

"We'll be sure to do that. Thanks for your cooperation, sir," Red said.

"My pleasure, Dr. Quincy."

Dan walked into the room followed by Red. Dan began searching through the suitcases, the same suitcases he had seen in Tess's hotel room the week before. Red searched through the nightstand, and dresser drawers.

"What exactly are we looking for?" Red asked.

"I have no idea," Dan admitted. "I hope we'll know when we see it."

"See what?"

"Exactly."

After about twenty minutes they concluded their search, finding nothing that might tell them anything they wanted to know. As they walked out the door Dan noticed a garbage can on the sidewalk outside Garvey's door. He took off the lid and dumped the contents out onto the concrete walkway. As he kicked his foot through the papers, and empty potato chip packages, something caught his eye. He bent over and brushed some more paper aside to reveal a small leather holster. Dan saw the clerk getting a soda out of the vending machine and shouted.

"Hey! When was this garbage can emptied last?"

"This morning," replied the startled clerk. "They empty them every morning."

Dan rubbed his chin and said, "Garvey's got a gun, Red. He didn't happen to mention that the other day. He must have thrown the holster in here on his way out the door."

"Why would he throw the holster away?"

"How would I know? I'm no mind reader. Maybe he likes to put the gun in his waistband like they do in the movies. I hear some guys like to do that."

"Where do you think he was going?"

"My bet is on the Laguna Inn. Let's head over there."

"Should we call for back up, Detective Fish?"

"Shut up and get in the car, Quincy."

Chapter Thirty-Four

Dan and Red pulled up in front of the Laguna Inn, in the exact same place Dan had parked the day before. Right in front of his car, was Garvey's car.

"Well, he's here all right." Red said. "What now?"

"Open the glove box," Dan said.

Red did as Dan asked. Seeing the gun surprised Red. He didn't know if he was ready for an encounter that might involve flying lead.

"Uh, Dan, why do you have a gun?"

"Just in case."

"If you get me killed, I'll never speak to you again."

"Don't threaten me with a reward, Red. Come on, let's go around back. There's windows in each room overlooking the pool. Let's see if we can get a look in Hinder's room."

Dan placed the gun in his waistband, and the two men headed toward the hotel pool. They quietly opened the gate. Dan motioned Red in first, and then followed. There was no one at the stagnant pool, of course. Both men crouched down and made their way up to the window.

The curtain was pulled back just enough to see in. Garvey was standing in the middle of the room, pointing his gun at Hinder. Hinder was tying Karen to a chair with a roll of duct tape. Dan recognized the tape, and he recognized the binding job. He grinned a little on the inside. *Karma's a bitch*, he thought. *She better hope there's not a tequila bottle nearby.*

"The bastard stole my duct tape," Dan whispered to Red.

Dan and Red knelt quietly and watched. They could hear Garvey and Hinder talking, but couldn't make out what they were saying. It was obvious that both men thought the other might know where the money was.

"Peeping Tom, peeping Tom!" came a screeching voice behind them.

Startled, Dan and Red spun around to see an elderly bag lady. She waived a cane in one hand, while the other gripped a plastic bag bulging with aluminum cans. Her yelling turned her face the same shade of blue as her hair.

"*Shhhhhh*," Dan whispered to the woman, with a finger to his lips. "*Shhhhhh.*"

"Peeping tom!" she yelled out again.

"Go away, ya crazy old bag!" Red whisper-yelled and lifted the back of Dan's shirt just enough to reveal the gun. The woman's eyes widened; she turned and hurried back the way she had come.

"What a nice surprise," Garvey said.

Dan and Red slowly looked to their right and upward. Tim Garvey was standing in the doorway with his .38 Smith and Wesson revolver pointing right at them.

"Come on in and join the party," Garvey said, motioning them inside.

Dan and Red exchanged a pained *oh shit* look, rose, and went into the hotel room at a dead man walking pace. Dan looked around the room. There was a table to the right of the door. Sitting on the table was an empty pizza box. There were three chairs next to the table. One chair was occupied by Jeff Hinder, and Karen was duct taped to the other. There were two beds to the left of the door, both unmade. There was also a front door to the room that exited to the parking lot. Dan looked at Karen. She struggled at her bonds. Across her mouth was a length of duct tape.

"Are you screwing these guys too, because they're not dishwashers you know?" Dan asked.

Karen mumbled something from under the duct tape. Hinder spoke for her.

"She's my sister, you moron!"

Red look confused. "You know these two?"

"Yeah," Dan answered. "He *hit* me in the head, and she *gave* me head. They're both good at what they do."

Hinder rose, fists clenched to confront Dan.

Garvey pointed his gun at Hinder. "Sit down!" Hinder did as he was told.

Garvey turned the weapon back to Dan and Red. "You gentlemen have a seat as well."

Red looked around and protested, "There's only one chair,"

"One of you sit on the bed, then!" Garvey shouted.

"Which bed?" Dan asked.

"I don't care, just sit!"

"Wow. You didn't mention how rude this guy was," Red muttered as he plopped down on the bed.

"So, what are you gonna do now, Garvey?" Dan demanded. "Shoot us all? You're not a killer. You're not like Hinder."

"I didn't kill anyone," Hinder said evenly.

Dan looked him straight in the eye. "Are you forgetting about Garvey's wife?"

"I didn't kill Tess, dammit! I was here, with my sister, that night." Hinder's voice grew manic; he leveled a trembling finger at Garvey. "He did it, he killed Tess! I loved her!"

"Loved her? She was my wife. *My wife!*" Garvey yelled. "You took her away from me, you bastard."

Dan waited a moment for the tension to die down and addressed Garvey. "So, you killed her."

"I didn't mean to. She just made me so angry," Garvey replied in a weary monotone. "She told me she gave you the money for safekeeping. She said it was at your house. She said I could have it all. She just wanted me to leave her and Jeff alone. She told me she loved him. She wanted to be with him, not me. I was so angry. I grabbed her by the arms, she tried to pull away ...I lost grip on her ...She slipped and fell and hit her head. I was just trying to scare her. I wanted her to change her mind."

"So it was an accident," Dan said. "You can still let us go. There's still a way out of this for you."

Garvey shook his head. "No one will believe me, that it was an accident."

"So what are you gonna do now?" Dan asked.

"I don't have a choice. I have to go to your house and get the money. I can't leave you all here alive. As soon as I leave, you'll start yelling, someone will hear you."

"The money's not there, Garvey," Dan said.

Garvey's face said he didn't believe him. "She said it was."

Garvey walked over to the table and picked up the roll of duct tape he tossed it to Red, and pointed at Dan.

"Tie him up," Garvey ordered. "Hands behind his back."

Red got up from the bed and walked around behind Dan. Obediently, Dan put his hands behind his back. Red bent over, secretly lifting Dan's shirt tail. Red pulled the end of the duct tape, making the familiar farting sound that everyone knows so well. In one deft motion he dropped the tape and grabbed the gun. Quick as a fox Dan leaned forward out of the line of fire. Red came up with the gun in his hand. Garvey fired first, hitting Red in the right shoulder. Red fired and hit Garvey in the chest, just as Garvey's .38 barked a second time. Garvey fell back onto the bed, dropping his gun. Dan rose up, grabbing his gun from Red. Jeff Hinder jumped from his chair and seized Garvey's gun from the floor. He spun around to see his only sister staring helplessly at him. Garvey's second bullet had found her neck. She was choking up blood from behind the duct tape. Her eyes fluttered and closed; her head dropped to her chest.

"You bastards!" Hinder yelled, turning his weapon toward Dan and Red. Dan fired twice. Once into Hinder's stomach, and once into his head.

Dan looked back at his friend and saw the blood dripping down his arm to the floor.

"I suppose you're never going to talk to me again," Dan said.

Red waved a dismissive hand. "I'm not dead yet."

Dan hurried over to Hinder's body and dragged it back to the chair. He picked up the .38 and walked over to Garvey's body, wiped any prints with Garvey's shirt tail, and placed the gun in Garvey's hand. He then took his own gun off the table, wiped it off in the same manner, and placed it in Hinder's hand. He then went to the bathroom and washed his hands and brought Red a washcloth to do the same. After Red was finished. Dan took the washcloth and threw it into the bathtub and grabbed a towel for Red's wound. He then walked over to the chair next to his friend, handed him the towel, and sat down. He reached back and picked up his duct tape.

"I guess we better get you to the hospital." Dan said.

"Unless you brought a needle and thread." Red responded.

Just then they heard a car pull into the parking lot, then another, and then another. They could see the lights of the cop cars reflected off the mirror above the dresser. Two silhouettes ran by the window. A loud voice rang out over a bullhorn. It was Rick.

"We have the place surrounded. Come out with your hands up!"

"They really say that?" Red asked Dan.

"I have a feeling just Rick says that. Rick, and maybe Barney Fife," Dan said as they both laughed. "I guess we better get our story straight."

"Orgy gone bad?" Red suggested.

"How about, we came here looking for Hinder, right in the middle of their argument over who killed Tess? Hinder professed his love for Tess, Garvey shot Karen, and then Garvey and Hinder shot each other."

Red nodded. "That's what I saw. What about the money?"

Dan raised one eyebrow. "What money?"

At that moment one of Rick's officers kicked in the front door, as another smashed through the back door. Several officers charged into the room, guns drawn in the two-fisted Weaver stance and pointed in every direction. Rick was the last officer to enter the room. He tried to hide his surprise as he saw Dan and Red sitting in their chairs.

"What are you two doing here?" He demanded.

"Pizza party," Dan said, pointing at the empty box on the table.

"Orgy gone bad," Red said.

"That's them, that's the two peeping Toms, officer!" The old woman hid behind Rick's ample girth pointing her knobby finger at two seated men.

"Jimmy, please escort this woman out of the room," Rick said to one of the officers. "and get those EMTs in here for Red."

"It's just a scratch," Red said. "it's almost stopped bleeding already."

As the EMTs assisted Red to the ambulance, Dan gave Rick his version of what had transpired. He told Rick how Garvey confessed to Tess's murder. He told him about Garvey's faked death. Dan didn't mention the insurance money. Dan figured if Rick wanted the complete story, he should do the work himself, but Dan knew he wouldn't.

"Well then, I guess this murder is solved," Rick said.

"I guess so," Dan agreed.

"But don't leave town. I might have a few more questions for you."

"Where would I go?"

Chapter Thirty-Five

Dan and Alex stood in the backyard next to the fire pit, looking out at the ocean. They were holding hands as they always did. Alex snuggled up to Dan and kissed his cheek.

"Well, Boobers, what do you think, should we do it?" she asked.

Dan turned toward the real estate agent who had followed them through the house, around the yard, and was now standing behind them.

"Mrs. Dixon?" Dan asked.

"Yes, Mr. Coast?"

"Do the two Adirondack chairs come with the house? I have a feeling we're going to get a lot of use out of them."

"Yes, Mr. Coast, I think they do."

"Then you have yourself a deal."

*****

Dan awoke. It was the morning after the fateful encounter at the Laguna. He lay in his bed staring up at the slowly spinning ceiling fan. He thought of Alex. He thought of her smile. He thought of everything they had wanted to do. Eleven years of smiles, conversations, kisses, lovemaking, and happiness ran through his mind in a matter of seconds. They say almost dying makes your whole life flash before your eyes. No one ever tells you that someone else dying makes two people's lives flash before your eyes every day for the rest of your life. Dan Coast got out of bed and got dressed.

As he walked from his bedroom to his living room, he saw Red coming up the front steps. Dan hadn't closed the door the night before. Security is an afterthought when you're drunk.

"Coffee, Red?"

"That would be great."

"How's the shoulder?"

"Fine. Just grazed me. Only six stitches."

Dan poured them each a cup of yesterday's coffee and heated it up in the microwave. They walked out the back door and down the gravel pathway to the lawn chairs.

"Good morning, neighbor!" Bev called from her back porch, holding her own cup of coffee in the air.

"Good morning, Bev," Dan yelled back. "Come on over and join us!"

Bev did just that. The three of them sat in companionable silence drinking their coffee and taking turns reading sections of Bev's morning paper.

"Hey, did you read this, Dan?" Bev said, pointing at front-page article. "Looks like there was a shooting over at the Laguna Inn. Three people dead. I tell ya, that place is no good. Attracts the wrong kind of element."

"You don't say," Red replied.

"Some guy shot a woman and then the two guys shot each other. Why would someone do that?" Bev asked.

"Maybe the room service sucked, maybe his mattress wasn't comfortable," Red said, grinning at Dan.

"Yeah, maybe his mattress was…" Dan paused, staring blankly.

"What's the matter, Dan?" Red asked.

Red and Bev stared at Dan. Without a word he stood up and walked up the gravel pathway toward his back door, up the steps, and into his kitchen. He stood in the doorway between the kitchen and living room staring at Buddy, who was trying to get comfortable on his bed.

"What's the matter, pal, can't get comfortable?" Dan asked.

Dan slowly walked to Buddy's bed. Buddy stepped to one side. Dan knelt down and unzipped the dog bed. There it was, stuffed in Buddy's bed. Where it had been since the morning Tess put it there, before waking Dan, who was sleeping off a hangover in his hammock. Dan reached his hand into the mattress and pulled out a small stack of cash, banded together with adhesive currency band that read $5,000.00. He reached his hand back in and pulled out more. It was all there.

He stood up and walked to the back door. Bev and Red were still seated in their chairs chatting away, unaware of Dan's find.

"Hey! I'm gonna have to cut the morning short," Dan yelled out the back door. "I have some things I have to take care of today. I'll catch up with you two later."

Dan closed the door and went to his bedroom to grab a duffel bag out of the closet. He counted out three hundred thousand dollars and put it in the bag. The remainder of the money he took to his closet and put it beneath the loose floorboard.

Dan returned to the living room. Buddy, fast asleep, had finally been able to get comfortable on his bed. From his contented look and the twitching of his legs, Dan figured the dog was dreaming about chasing a ball on the beach. A ball probably thrown by Alex.

Dan decided not to wake him, but tomorrow morning he promised himself that the dog deserved steak for breakfast. And Red would probably be getting a large tip.

Chapter Thirty-Six

Dan, showered and shaven, threw the duffel bag into the passenger seat of his Porsche, and wasted no time getting out of Dodge. He drove down his street to the stop sign, took a left, drove a few blocks, and then took a right onto US-1.

As he drove, he pulled his cell phone from his pocket, searched his contacts, and dialed. A woman answered.

"Hello?"

"Candi?"

"Yes?"

"It's Dan. I'm going to be in town for a couple of days. I was wondering if we could get together."

"That would be great! I was hoping you would call. When will you be here?"

"I'll be in Miami at about one. I have to deliver something to a guy first. Then I'll give you a call."

Dan Coast pressed end call on his cell phone and tossed it onto the duffel bag next to him. He turned on his radio and tuned it to Radio Margaritaville. Jimmy was singing about surfing in a hurricane. Dan sang along with Jimmy.

The End

Don't miss the next Dan Coast Tale

Ocean Floors

Available May, 2013

Here's a preview

Dan Coast opened his eyes to the sound of a naked woman looking for her underwear, whatever *that* sound is. She was forty, maybe forty-five. Who knows these days? Everyone woman under sixty tries to look twenty. Her skin was tanned. Not too tanned. No tan lines. She was holding a pair of faded jeans, the kind with pre-made, thread bare holes. Twenty-five years ago she probably wore a pair just like them to a Bon Jovi, or Poison concert. Ten years ago she would have scoffed at any woman wearing a pair. Now, doing as the magazines and the *Style Network* have told her, she's wearing them again.

Draped over her left forearm she had a white wife beater, probably not Hanes, or Fruit of the Loom. Hollister probably, or American Eagle. Whichever store made her feel younger that day. Whichever store had a young good-looking salesclerk who was smart enough to say, "Wow, forty? Really? You don't look forty. I would have guessed twenty-eight, maybe twenty-nine."

In the same hand she held a pair of pink Adidas sneakers, running shoes. From the looks of those legs, she used those running shoes quite a bit. She walked around the carpet on her tiptoes, which made the muscles in her calves stand out. *Nice*, Dan thought.

With the other arm she was doing her best to cover her large, fake, tanned breasts.

Great job on the boobs.

There was a slight scar underneath each breast. He hadn't noticed that last night, but then again with the amount of tequila that was consumed he probably wouldn't have noticed a conjoined twin hanging off the front of her.

"Where's my bra and panties?" she asked furiously.

Dan didn't answer. He just lay there enjoying the show and wondered why she was making such an attempt to cover up those beautiful breasts. After all, there was no part of her he hadn't seen just a few short hours before. Another thing, why did she choose to cover up the breasts and not the lower, well groomed, goodies. Women always make out that it's more taboo to see the lower than the upper, but when faced with the decision, always seem to cover the upper. After all, on this particular specimen, it was the lower section that told the hidden truth. She wasn't really blonde; she was a red head. *Carpet don't match the drapes,* Dan thought. He was grinning on the inside. It was probably best at this point that she does not see him smiling.

"Can you help me? God! What was I thinking? This was a mistake." She cried out.

Ouch! Mistake?

"…and you better erase those pictures from last night, Coast.

Dan was smiling on the outside now. He remembered his camera on the nightstand. He remembered the manila envelope containing the pictures he was paid to take two weeks earlier. He also remembered the few photos he took in the room last night. He took those for free…

Made in the USA
Columbia, SC
15 June 2024